The Christmas Storm

TUCKAWAY BAY
BOOK THREE

MADELEINE JAIMES

SAND DUNE BOOKS

The Christmas Storm

Tuckaway Bay, Book 3

Madeleine Jaimes

Learn more about Madeleine Jaimes at www.maddiejamesbooks.com

Join the VIP Newsletter List at Newsletter – Maddie James Books

Dedication

To mothers. To daughters.

The Christmas Storm

They said it would be a quiet Christmas at the beach.

When a Nor'easter sweeps into the coastal town of Tuckaway Bay on Christmas Eve, the residents and guests of Sea Glass Inn prepare to hunker down and weather the storm. But which is worse—the storm raging outside, or the one brewing _inside_ the inn?

***

Having survived their first year of running Sea Glass Inn—and a year of marriage—Zach and Lia Allen decide to celebrate the holidays by inviting their friends back to Tuckaway Bay for the Christmas holiday weekend.

Wait. Correction.

Zach reluctantly agrees. He really wants a quiet Christmas alone with Lia.

Of course, there is plenty of room at the inn for Lia's girlfriends—even though half of the rooms are closed down for deep cleaning and painting—but what about the children and significant others? Not to mention Zach's friends from New Hampshire who crash the inn after the Nor'easter cancels their winter fishing expedition.

As if space is the only issue...

Is the resort large enough to handle fluctuating family dynamics, teenage angst, pregnancy hormones, and perimenopausal women? Can Sea Glass Inn, and its guests, survive the mood swings and hot flashes?

Fa-la-la-la-la. Let the reindeer games begin!

Lia & Belle

One

MAY

IF SHE DIDN'T KNOW ANY BETTER, SHE'D SWEAR SOMEONE was watching her.

Ridiculous.

It was a feeling more than anything. But Belle Mitchell's common sense told her to keep her head down, her arms moving, and her legs propelling her body forward in the water.

Three laps.

Four.

Ten.

Twenty.

She'd flip at each turn of the pool and expertly push herself away from the edge, gliding into her workout routine.

Freestyle.

Breaststroke.

Backstroke.

Butterfly.

Still feels like someone's eyes are on me.

When she swam competitively in high school and college, she would shut out everyone and everything around her when she was in the zone. With every turn, her determination grew stronger and the only thing she could think about was touching the other side of the pool wall before anyone else.

That was all that mattered.

Then.

Today, she was simply out for an early morning swim—an enjoyable workout to keep her swimming muscles toned and tuned, while simultaneously providing therapy for her leg. The exercise was also good for her heart.

Zach kept the pool lights on all night for security reasons, which was good for her—she could swim uninterrupted before most people were up. Beach vacation getaways make for lazy wake-up calls at the Sea Glass Inn Resort, so she knew she could easily get her laps in without dodging guests before work.

Her day started early now that she oversaw guest reservations for the Inn. Over the past year, her mother had taken on more responsibilities in the resort's management—finances, accounting, payroll, event and catering bookings, and so forth. Zach, of course, was the CEO and general manager, but he also oversaw maintenance, the restaurant and tiki bar, and housekeeping.

Belle had gradually taken over reservations, which she liked. It gave her an opportunity to chat with potential customers before they arrived, and then greet them when they did. She prided herself on remembering some details about their trips, and always tried to be helpful when guests had questions—like where to get a good seafood boil, or the best place to windsurf, how to get tickets to the Lost Colony outdoor drama, or what time the ferries ran down at Cape Hatteras.

Since she had only taken college classes part-time last semester, mostly online, she explored and learned more about the area so she could give the guests correct and useful information.

She almost felt like she knew the guests before they arrived.

Basically, she was the Sea Glass Inn concierge, and she was very much okay with that.

That's why, when she pushed up out of the pool and reached for her towel on a nearby lounge chair, and spotted the guy across the way watching her, she knew he wasn't a guest.

Seriously, if he *were* a guest, she would have remembered him.

He was that cute.

Tall and fit, the guy stood arms crossed, a shock of hair falling over his forehead, leaning against the sliding glass door of an ocean-level suite. He met her gaze—a soft breeze lazily lifting that sun kissed length of hair from his eyes, once and again.

"Hey."

Belle lowered her goggles, letting them hang around her neck. Green. His eyes were green underneath those shaggy blond bangs. "Hey back." She continued to dry off.

"Early bird, I see."

"Yes." She eyed him, raising her head and straightening. "You're not a guest here."

"That right?"

"Yes, that's right. This is private property." She ran the towel over her face and hair.

"So you say."

"I do." She paused, eyeing him, a bit annoyed by the devil-may-care glint in his eye. His slouch against the door frame reminded her of James Dean in an old movie she'd watched with her mother once. "What's your name?"

He shrugged. "Not important. Just thought I'd say hey." He turned inward, heading inside the room.

"Whoa. Wait." She stepped forward.

He stalled for a few seconds, then looked back. "What?"

"You're not a guest."

He squared his body, facing her. "Actually, I am. Arrived late last night."

Belle wracked her brain trying to remember who was staying in suite 106. A young couple. Lucy and Alex Cooper. Recently married.

"You know the Coopers?" she asked.

"Lucy is my sister."

Okay. Well... I can't imagine why anyone would invite their brother to their honeymoon, but okay. She peered around him, but of course couldn't see into the darkened suite through the closed door. "And they are...?"

"Sleeping. In the bedroom. I crashed on the pullout sofa."

"I see." But she didn't. Not really.

"Kind of nosy, aren't you? Is that why you get up so early? To nose around?"

"I could ask you the same question. Most guests are still in bed."

He chuckled. "And are you counted as one of those?"

"One of those what?"

"Guests."

Belle sighed. *Goodness. Now who's nosy?* "That's none of your business."

"I see."

"All that splashing around woke me up, you know."

"Really now. Interesting." It was an excuse, and she knew it. Belle wasn't a splashy swimmer. In fact, she worked hard to swim her laps with as little splash as possible.

She looked him over.

He stared back. "So, I'll ask again, what are you doing out here so early?"

Tiring of the dialogue, Belle wrapped the towel around her waist and glared. "Well, I'm not making tamales. What does it look like I'm doing?"

"Swimming."

"So smart of you."

"You do this every morning? Because I need to make sure I get my beauty sleep."

Belle huffed...but also inwardly smiled. "I do. So plan for it."

He took a couple of steps forward. "And *why* do you swim every morning?"

Giving him what she hoped was a sassy grin, rather than a saucy one, she replied, "Because I'm a swimmer." *Dummy. What do you think?*

"Oh, like in the Olympics?" he prodded.

"Not the Olympics. I will never swim in the Olympics."

"Too bad. You're good."

"Thanks. I appreciate your expert evaluation."

"Anytime."

She turned and took a few steps, shaking her head. The guy was cute but a whole lot of arrogant. As soon as she'd get to her desk, she'd check in with the Coopers to make sure everything was on the up and up.

"You must compete or something. Swim team?"

To be honest, this conversation was getting annoying. She glanced back. "I swim because I have done that for almost every day of my life since I was three years old. It's what I do. It's good exercise. It's great for my lungs, my heart, and my leg."

"Your leg. What's wrong with your leg?"

Belle glanced down and dropped her towel. "Nothing now. Swimming is physical therapy."

She watched his gaze slide down her right leg, thigh to ankle, lingering on her kneecap.

He whistled. "Man, that's some scar."

"Two breaks, femur and ankle. Shattered kneecap. Three surgeries."

"Well, you're gonna have to tell me *that* story one day," he said.

"Right. Probably not."

"Not into swapping war wound stories?"

She turned fully and faced him. "Look. I doubt we'll have many more conversations after today, so no. Not telling the story."

"All right. What did you say your name was again?"

"I didn't."

He crossed his arms, feigning a questioning expression on his face. "Really? I could swear...."

"Doesn't matter since we will not see each other again."

"You are a feisty one, aren't you?"

"Takes one to know one, so they say."

"Whoa!" He laughed. "Sarcasm and sass. I like that."

Belle shook her head, rolled her eyes, and sauntered off toward the hotel. "Go get some sleep," she called over her shoulder. "I swim early every day."

He watched her walk away. She knew this, even though she didn't turn around. His gaze was definitely following her as she entered the hotel multi-purpose room—much like when he'd watched her swimming earlier.

———

Two hours later, after a shower and breakfast, Belle settled in at her desk and opened the bookings software. Scanning the current reservations, she searched for suite 106. The Coopers had listed two guests in the room and were checking out on Monday. That meant they would be there two more nights—Saturday and Sunday.

Picking up the phone, she dialed 106 and a sleepy woman answered. "Hello?"

"Good morning, Mrs. Cooper," she began. "This is Belle at the front desk. My apologies for calling so early."

She heard some rustling about, possibly bed linens and pillows. "Everything alright?"

"Oh yes, we believe so. This is a courtesy call. There was a young man at your room door this morning in the pool patio area. He said he was in room 106. You don't have a third guest listed on your reservation, so we wanted to make sure everything was on the up and up."

"Oh, yes." Lucy Cooper sighed. "My brother, Chad. It was an unexpected visit, but he was in the area for work, so he's spending the weekend. I'm so sorry I didn't tell you, but it happened quickly."

Ah, I see. "It's no problem, Lucy. We just want to keep you safe, and the resort private. Checking on incidents like this is one way we do that."

"Well, thank you. Do I need to add his name to our reservation?"

Belle shook her head as though Lucy could see her. "I'll just note a third guest. Don't forget to remind him about the free breakfast bar and coffee in the multipurpose room until ten. Thanks so much and I hope you can get back to sleep."

"No worries. We're driving down to Ocracoke today, so we need to get moving, anyway."

"Have a safe trip. Oh, and if you want a good place to eat, try Jason's. It's on the edge of town."

"Fabulous. Thanks, Belle."

"You're welcome."

She cradled the landline phone with a sigh of relief. The mystery guest might have indeed been arrogant and annoying, but at least he was legit. That task done, she busied herself for the next couple of hours, confirming online reservations and returning inquiry calls to potential guests. The fall bookings were filling up fast.

"You're making a lot of calls this morning."

Belle looked up and met her mother's smile from across the room. Lia had slipped in earlier while she was on the phone. Her mom's desk sat on the opposite side of the office, facing Belle's.

"Morning, Mom. Yes, a few. If everyone who has called asking about vacancies books rooms, we will be at capacity for the summer and through October. I can't believe how quickly the fall weeks are selling out."

"That's a good problem to have, though," Lia said. "Zach will be pleased."

"I'm sure."

"You've held the last week of August for beach week, right?"

Belle nodded. "Tequila Sunrise is back in commission, so I've held it for that week. That's what you wanted, right? To stay at the beach house instead of the cottages?"

"Yes. We love that house."

Smiling, she gave her mother a nod. Lia and her friends had been staying at the Tequila Sunrise beach house for years, same week in August, ever since they were in college. Last year the house was under renovation, so they stayed at the resort, in the Gull Cottage. Belle knew there would be hell to pay if she let that reservation slide.

"No way would I book that house to someone else for the official beach week."

Her mother tossed her a grin. "Great." She rose then, heading for the door. "I need to catch Zach before he leaves. I think he has some receipts he's not given to me. See you after lunch."

"Bye, Mom." She gave her a wave, then turned back to her computer. After a few seconds, she heard footsteps approaching her desk. "Forget something?"

A male voice responded. "Yes. Your name."

Turning in her chair, she glanced up.

Ah. The infamous Chad. "Oh. You."

"Yes. Me."

"May I help you?"

He glanced about. "So, you work here?"

With a sigh, Belle sat back in her chair and eyed the handsome, somewhat sexy, but annoying dude who was taking up entirely too much space in her office area at this moment. "Yes, I work here, and I have a full day of work ahead of me, so I'll ask again—may I help you with something?"

"Belle Mitchell."

"Excuse me?"

"That's your name. Right?"

"What do you want?"

He leaned slightly to his right and picked up her name plate sitting on the desk. He fiddled with it for a few seconds, then replaced it. She said nothing.

Then his gaze met hers and, without warning, her cheeks heated—and her heart suddenly crashed against her chest wall. *What the hell?*

"Lucy says you're great at providing suggestions for guests. You know, good places to eat and things to do around here."

Nodding, she said, "That's my job."

"I'm in the mood for a good seafood buffet tonight. Nothing too fancy. Something down home with a local flavor. Lots of food, maybe some music, and great beer. Maybe craft. Suggestions?"

She could rattle off a ton of them but landed on her favorite. Maybe if she'd tell him, he would leave, and she could get back to work.

And settle her still thrumming heart.

"Bojo's Beach Buffet over on the sound is what you are looking for."

"Great. Can you give me an address?"

"Sure." She reached for her notepad, jotted down the street address, and handed it to him. She'd shared that restaurant hundreds of times, so she knew the address by heart.

He took the slip of paper.

And just stood there.

"Anything else?"

"I hate to eat alone."

Oh no. We're not going there. She stayed silent.

"Care to join me? Say, seven o'clock?"

Belle tilted her head slightly and eyed him. "I'm busy—but thank you." It wasn't a lie. She had plans with her girlfriends for this evening, even though for much later than seven.

"I see."

"Well, enjoy the food. I need to get back to work." She turned to her laptop and listened for his footsteps heading toward the door. She didn't hear them.

"If you change your mind...."

"If I change my mind," Belle glanced over her shoulder, "which I am not likely to do, I know where I can find you."

He nodded, holding her gaze momentarily. "I'll be at Bojo's at seven."

"Right."

Then he left.

BELLE INTENTIONALLY WAITED UNTIL AFTER ONE O'CLOCK that afternoon to grab lunch from the Sandcastle. She was hoping to avoid Chad, in case he was there.

Not that he was so annoying she couldn't get past it—she could, she supposed. What was so annoying was how he'd made her flush—and hopefully not physically blush—when he was standing by her desk eyeing her.

She couldn't deny he was a good-looking guy. Attractive. He was already tan, and it was only mid-May. His sun-bleached hair and dark green eyes were an interesting combination. He looked like the kind of guy who spent a lot of time outdoors.

Earlier, it was almost as though his stare had penetrated through to her pounding heart.

So avoiding him at all costs was a good thing.

Canoodling with the guests was a strict rule of Zach's—for all staff and employees—and she would not break it. Not that rule or any other rule. She respected Zach's wishes, and her mother's, immensely. Plus, she didn't want to risk losing the job she loved so much.

A housekeeper had gotten fired last month for doing the naughty with a guest.

"Belle!" Her friend, Jenn, one of the wait staff, waved her over. "I just cleaned a table by the window if you want it. What can I get for you?"

Belle joined her. "I'll just get something to go. BLT and chips, please? Oh, and a diet soda."

"Gotcha. Have a seat if you want, and I'll get your order in."

Sitting at the end of the counter, Belle risked a glance about the restaurant. It was pretty full still, but she didn't see Chad. Immediately, she let go of the breath that she'd obviously been holding for a while. Her chest relaxed with the released breath.

He was cute. And, even though intrigued by his devil-may-care ways, that was also an issue for her. She preferred stable, grounded men. Besides, he'd be gone by Monday. No good ever came from a weekend hookup. Right? That was not her style.

Jenn returned and placed a to-go cup of diet soft drink in front of her. "Still on for tonight?"

She nodded, reaching for a straw and peeling off the paper. "Yes! Cammie still coming?"

"No." Jenn shook her head and frowned. "I just got a text. She's back with Marcus so they are going out."

Belle rolled her eyes. "Those two. They need to either tie the knot or let it go."

"I know."

A couple entered the restaurant and Jenn glanced their way. "I need to seat these people and check my tables. Melissa said she'll bring out your sandwich. In case I don't catch you again, I'll meet you out by the Party Pier at nine."

"Okay! Bye."

Melissa, the kitchen manager, came with the to-go order quickly and Belle headed back to her desk. She had tons of work—hopefully she could concentrate on it. Fortunately, the afternoon flew, and later that evening, she drove to the sound-side pier to meet Jenn.

She glanced curiously at Bojo's as she passed the restaurant, which was a few blocks down from Tri-B and the pier.

The Party Pier was actually a dock with a large gazebo bar that jutted out into a shallow part of the bay, on the backside of the Bay Beach Bistro restaurant—or the Tri-B as it was known locally. The pier was a favorite partying spot with the local college-age crowd. Since it was on the sound side of the island, not a lot of vacationers came over—which was fine with the locals.

The Tri-B was also a great seafood restaurant, but she had intentionally *not* told Chad about it because, for one, it also catered heavily to locals, and two, she knew she'd be there tonight. The last thing she wanted was for him to think she was chasing after him, or something.

Because she definitely wasn't.

Not by a long shot.

"Belle!"

She spotted Jenn waving across the parking lot. She hugged her when they drew closer and linked arms as they slipped down the dock and into the gazebo bar. Before she knew it, she was on her second Island Mojito, and she and Jenn were laughing and dancing to an indie rock band from Richmond.

When the music stopped, she took a minute to catch her breath and told Jenn she was heading for another drink.

"That guy is staring at you," Jenn told her.

"What?" She was a little tipsy and still out of breath from dancing.

"That guy by the exit. He hasn't taken his eyes off you since he stepped into the gazebo."

Belle turned and squinted. It was dark, of course, and there were strobe lights blinking and pulsing around them, and her brain was slightly fuzzy... But after a moment, her vision cleared, and she got a good look at him.

Mostly because he was walking steadily toward her.

"Shit." She grasped Jenn's hand. "Let's go."

"Hell no!" Jenn removed her hand and pushed her toward the guy. "He's a cutie."

He sauntered their way and stopped before Belle, looking down at her with a crooked, *one-corner-of-his-mouth-turned-up* grin that made her blood burn almost down to her toes.

Hell. Who was she kidding? Her toes were practically curling with sizzle.

"Well. Belle Mitchell. As I live and breathe."

She nodded. "Chad."

"You know my name."

"I have ways."

He put his hand out. "Dance?"

She gave a quick glance at Jenn, who nodded back urgently, then again at Chad. "Oh, what the hell." She grasped his hand. "See if you can keep up with me."

The annoying Chad grabbed her hand, tugged her into his arms—and then totally and completely swept Belle Mitchell off her feet.

Two

September

Lia Allen watched her daughter methodically swim her morning laps from their third-floor apartment deck. Recently, Belle had shortened her routine to about thirty minutes a day, and was now skipping Tuesday and Thursday mornings.

That was worrisome.

When Lia had questioned her about it, Belle blew her off with some half-thought-out excuse about how hot it was, or that she'd pulled a muscle.

Lia didn't believe it for a minute.

Searching beyond the pool and beach, her gaze settled on the sun just cresting the Atlantic horizon, shooting yellows and reds and pinks into the hazy blue-gray sky. Instantly reminded of how fortunate they were to live in Tuckaway Bay, and at this resort, she sighed and brushed away her uneasy feelings.

It had been a while since she'd watched Belle swim for any length of time—not since she swam competitively in high school. After Belle had gone to college in Washington state, Lia hadn't visited yet to catch a meet, before the terrible bus accident that changed everything.

And even now as she watched her daughter, observing her smooth, rhythmic, and deliberate strokes, her agile body gliding through the water, she knew that Belle had been fortunate. The night the team bus skidded off the icy mountain road in Idaho could have turned catastrophic for her and the family.

Belle could have died. Her coach and a couple of teammates did. But she survived the accident with a badly broken leg—albeit a career-ending break—and for that, they'd all been grateful.

But that knowledge didn't calm her increasingly nagging concern of late—that heavy ache just below her breastbone that signaled things weren't quite right. While she couldn't put her finger on it, Lia sensed, knew, that something was going on with her daughter—even if Belle didn't realize it.

So, for days, she'd quietly observed, as Belle went on with her day.

Her girl seemed tired and had started going to bed earlier.

Her eating habits had changed—she wanted more food in the morning and a lighter dinner. She'd put on a few pounds, and her face and eyes looked puffy, swollen. At first, Lia thought that was from more hours of sleep, but now she wasn't so sure.

Was it her heart? They'd gone twenty years with little concern about Belle's congenital heart defect. Immediate surgery after birth had fixed the issues and her doctors were certain everything was fine—for then and the future. Annual physicals had always gone well, and she was pronounced strong and fit. The swimming had helped to strengthen not only her heart, but her lungs.

But now? Years later? Had some problem returned?

Perhaps she should call Ned Speakman, Belle's cardiologist at Chicago Med. Maybe they needed to make a trip back there, just to ease her mind. She'd call for an appointment later today and arrange for the trip. Surely, he would work them in—he was always booked so far in advance. But Ned had been long time friends of her family, so she hoped she could count on that.

As much as she didn't want to, she needed to discuss this with Belle.

Maybe she'd just tell her she wanted a mother-daughter week, back in Chicago, just the two of them, and they'd pop in to see Ned. She could probably pull that off since the season was slowing down. Zach could handle things. Right?

Looking down again, she watched her girl slowly climb the ladder at the end of the pool, wondering when she'd started doing that rather than pushing herself up out of the water to sit on the side of the pool. Belle had always had good upper body strength.

Suddenly, her chest ached with fear and concern, and she had to choke back tears.

Something was wrong with her baby.

No. She couldn't "trick" her into going to Chicago. They just had to do it.

The sun sinking behind the hotel sent warm orange rays of light into the apartment Belle shared with her mother and Zach. Pacing with a restless energy that seemed otherwise out of place, she clasped her hands together, tight at her abdomen. Her knuckles ached where her fingers intertwined.

All a sign of the storm of emotions brewing inside her chest.

She'd been keeping a secret for way too long.

Had her mother sensed something? Was that why she had asked to have a chat later today? Why she'd mentioned Chicago earlier, and how they had always loved it in the fall? And wouldn't she want to go back and visit?

Pausing at a window, Belle caught sight of her reflection—worry lines etched her face and her swollen eyes appeared clouded with uncertainty. She took a deep breath, then exhaled.

"You can do this, Belle," she whispered. "Just tell her."

The rhythmic beat of the ocean waves a few hundred yards away rivaled the erratic beating of her heart. She listened and tried to calm her rambling nerves.

Usually, the beach was her sanctuary. Not tonight.

"Everything okay, honey?" Her mother's concern cut through Belle's contemplation. "You look lost in thought."

Belle turned. Her mom stood in the doorway, watching. Her eyes, always a mirror of warmth, searched for something it seemed—perhaps the source of her unease? Quiet question marks lingered in the air between them.

"Hey, Mom." Her voice cracked a little. "I'm just...thinking. You know, about things, life stuff."

"Life stuff, huh?" Lia stepped further into the room, closing the distance between them.

She'd always had an easy way of doing that, building bridges rather than walls. But when Belle looked into her mother's eyes, she saw worry.

Her mom had always been there for her, through good and bad times. The divorce. Her accident. Why was she so concerned about how her mother would react to the information she was about to share?

"Anything you want to talk about? Are you feeling okay?"

Torn between the safe harbor of silence, the chaos of confession, and her doubts about the future, Belle hesitated. This was her mother— her lighthouse in every storm, the one who had always guided her home with enduring love and patience.

Still....

"Mom, I..." The words tangled on her tongue. She wanted to spill them out and hold onto them at the same time.

"You know you can talk to me, honey," her mother whispered. "Whatever it is, we'll figure it out together. We always do."

"I know, Mom."

Belle's heart thrummed in her chest. *A drumbeat of impending change?* That felt dramatic but in reality, it was true. Her life was about to change forever.

Still, she knew that no matter what, she had her mother's support.

Even if she was disappointed.

"I know something is going on. Belle. Please tell me. Are you okay?"

Belle inhaled, nodded, and held her mother's gaze. "Yes. I'm...not okay. Sort of. Something is going on."

A breath whooshed from Lia's mouth, and she deflated onto the sofa. Reaching for Belle's hand, she grasped it and tugged her down to sit beside her. "Oh, honey. Please tell me it's not your heart. I'm terrified."

Oh, please don't cry. Please don't, Mom!

The thought of her mother's greatest horror sent a tremor through Belle, and she knew she had to alleviate her mother's fear.

"No. No, Mom. It's not my heart."

"Oh, thank God." Relief washed over her mother's face.

Just do it, Belle. "It's something else."

"Tell me."

She nodded. "Last summer. Early in May, we had a guest here for the weekend. He wasn't a registered guest but the brother to a couple staying here."

Lia's eyes misted over again. "Did he hurt you? Oh, Belle...."

"No." She grasped her mother's hands. "Nothing like that."

"Okay."

"Mom. I'm...pregnant."

The confession rolled out, a tentative murmur, even though the words felt heavy on her tongue—a weight she'd carried alone for far too long.

For a moment, Lia's expression was unreadable, her eyes widening as if the world had shifted beneath her. But just as quickly, the surprise melted into a familiar resolve, the same determination that had seen them through late-night fevers and heart-to-heart talks in Chicago, and now in Tuckaway Bay.

"Oh, Belle," she uttered. "Sweetheart...."

Belle shook off a wave of nervous energy. "I'm sorry. I know you're disappointed in me."

"Come here." Her hands found Belle's shoulders, and she pulled her closer. Her mother's touch was solid and sure, and a welcome anchor for Belle's anxiety. "I'm not. Surprised, yes, but never disappointed."

"You're sure?"

"I am. Belle, honey. You're not alone, okay?"

"Okay."

"So what about this young man?"

Belle shook her head. "I can't find him."

"I see." They both fell silent for a few minutes.

"I did try."

"All right." Lia exhaled sharply. "You know you will need to tell

Zach. You are an employee of the resort and while this is a personal issue, you went against his wishes...."

"I know, the canoodling rule."

"It doesn't look good for business."

"I get that."

"Not that I am suggesting he do anything about it. And there is no reason this needs to be public knowledge. He just needs to know that you broke the rule."

"Not all the details though?" Belle searched her mother's eyes.

"Definitely not." She paused for a minute, then added, "So he did hurt you, in a way. This young man. By disappearing. Because Belle Mitchell, if there is one thing I know about you, you wouldn't have done this carelessly so you must have liked him, at least a little."

"I did like him, but I didn't really know him. I was careless and to be honest, I'm embarrassed by that."

"We all have those times, Belle."

Her breathing hitched at the matter-of-fact truth of her mother's words—and the kindness in her voice. In her mother's embrace, Belle found a lifeline back to herself, to the girl who once swam laps until the world blurred into nothing but the rhythm of her strokes—especially during the year of her parents' divorce. To the young woman Lia nursed back to health after the bus accident that took away her college swimming career.

Belle leaned into the embrace of Lia's support. She and Chad had had fun that night at the pier—she'd felt a connection, and he said he did too—and then the following evening, with the help of a little wine, she spent the night with him on the beach. She thought they'd shared an incredibly quick bond, and he'd promised he would call as soon as he got home, but then....

Nothing.

"Did you say May? That was over five months ago. Goodness, honey. Have you seen a doctor?" The words literally spilled out of her mother's mouth. "What about your heart? Oh, Belle. You can't risk this, can you? Have you considered...an abortion?"

"Mom! No. I have not considered an abortion. Besides, it's too late for that anyway. It's only legal in North Carolina the first twelve weeks."

"Unless there are complications. Your health. We still technically have a home in Chicago so...."

"Mom, no. There are no complications."

"But your heart!" Her mother's hands were literally shaking. "Oh sweetheart. What have you done? You can't have this baby."

Wait. No. Belle stood and backed away from the sofa. "I *can* have this baby, and I will."

Lia rose and followed her. "We need to call Chicago Med. I can do that for you. And you need to see an OB-GYN. We need to see Ned."

She blew out a shaking breath. "Mom, I've already taken care of all that! I've had two conference calls with Dr. Speakman and his cardiology team at Chicago Med. And, I've seen an obstetrician here every month since I found out. She—Dr. Christman—has also been part of the calls with the cardiologist. Dr. Speakman wants me to come to Chicago to run some tests, a physical, and lab work in a couple of weeks. I can stay at the condo."

"*We* can stay at the condo. I'll go with you."

Belle nodded. "I would like that."

"There is no way I would not go, honey."

"I know. Look, I don't want you to worry, Mom. I'm healthy. They see no risks. I'm following instructions—exercise, eating right, prenatal vitamins, regular checkups—and they continue to monitor all my vitals and the baby's. It's all good. Now, please, relax."

She let go of a deep sigh. "Okay, Grandma?"

Lia's eyes blinked rapidly, and Belle knew she was fighting tears. "Okay." Then in the next instant, the tears flowed. Her mother pulled her into her arms and grasped her so tight she could barely breathe.

"I love you so much, my sweet Belle," she whispered.

Now she was the one with tears in her eyes. "I know, Mom. I love you too."

If it was one thing Belle knew, though, her mother would be worried until the day she gave birth to her baby.

THE CLINK OF THE FRONT DOOR SIGNALED ZACH'S ARRIVAL, a soft buffer against the slight tension that had settled over the room. Lia stood by the open sliding glass door leading to the deck and turned as he entered. Belle sat on the edge of the sofa, hands clasped in her lap.

A sea breeze wafted inside, carrying a hint of sun-warmed salt into the room, but doing little to lessen the palpable unease.

While Belle insisted she was fine, Lia was, of course, worried.

Her daughter's life was about to change forever—and Lia wondered if Belle realized just how much.

"There are my girls." Zach's voice was the embodiment of calm, but Lia could tell that with one glance at the scene before him, he knew something was amiss. "Okay. What's wrong?"

"Belle has news."

"Alright. Is this something I need to know?" He crossed the room and sat beside Belle on the sofa.

"It's something that involves Belle," Lia told him. "You and me indirectly."

"Okay." He looked at Belle. "Are you all right?"

She nodded. "Mom already knows, but..." Belle's voice cracked a little.

Lia swallowed the lump in her throat. While she ached inside for her daughter, she knew Belle had to share this news with Zach. It's how she had always operated with Grant—she never covered up for her daughter, but insisted she own up to her own problems.

"I broke a rule, and... Zach, I'm sorry. I know the regulations about staff and guests, and it wasn't that I planned this—it just sort of happened. I shouldn't have let it happen, but I did. And now, well, I need to tell you because, hopefully it doesn't come back to bite the resort in the butt... I'm sorry. I'm rambling. I hope you are not mad at me."

Zach stared at her. "Belle, what in the world are you talking about?"

"I'm pregnant." The confession hung between them, fragile but also formidable. "I had a one-night fling with a guest. I'm fine. I've accepted it. I'm healthy. But you should fire me."

"Fire you?" Zach exchanged a glance with Lia. His expression tightened for a mere second, concern etching his features, then relaxed.

"It's not what I planned," Belle continued. "I'm sorry."

Zach took a breath. "Belle, I don't know what to say other than I'm not firing you."

"But what if other staff people find out? It's not fair to not fire me when you fired Jean Anne last week."

Shifting in his seat, Zach squared himself before her. "Look. Jean Anne was... Well, that's not important. Besides, that was an entirely different issue. People will eventually know you are pregnant, but no one needs to know the circumstances about how it happened. That's personal and your business."

"You know I don't want to do anything to hurt you and Mom, or the reputation of Sea Glass Inn."

"I'm not worried about that Belle," Zach replied. "I'm only worried about you."

"Ditto that," Lia interjected, settling next to Belle. "One thing at a time."

"Exactly," Zach chimed in. "We're family. And Sea Glass Inn? Well, according to stories I've heard from Aunt Grace, it's seen its share of scandals. This is just another part of its story."

Lia watched Belle's face turn from worry to amusement.

"I wish I'd known Aunt Grace."

"I do too, sweetie," Zach said. "She would have loved you, and your little one."

"Tell me the scandalous stories sometime?"

"Oh, definitely. But I have to warn you, they are a bit outrageous!"

"Ooh. Even better."

The smile that broke across Belle's face then lifted Lia's heart. It was the first smile she'd seen on her daughter in weeks. Getting her secret off her chest had apparently done wonders for her demeanor.

Her own chest heaved with an inhale, then deflated with a weighty sigh. In a few months, Belle would become a mother—and she and Zach would become grandparents.

That circle of life is rotating much too quickly.

Three

December

"Please tell me you are joking."

Lia glanced up from her desk and shrugged. Surely Zach didn't think she was kidding?

"I just thought we might like people around for the holidays," she explained. "Since my parents are staying in Chicago, and Aunt Grace is gone, I was thinking about a traditional family Christmas, but with friends. What do you think?"

Returning to her laptop and spreadsheet, she shuffled through some catering invoices from a wedding party they'd hosted the previous week.

"Seriously? You invited them all?"

He's not going to let this drop. Is he? She totaled the column of expenses, sighed, then gave him her full attention. "Yes. I invited them all."

"But Lia, this is our first Christmas together."

What? She met her husband's gaze. *That's the issue?* "Zach... We had Christmas together last year. I know it was busy, but we still had the holiday."

"Busy?" He sat in the chair opposite her desk. "Our apartment was torn up from the remodel, with construction workers in and out every day. Aunt Grace had passed a few weeks earlier, and we were still settling her estate. Plus, Belle was moving in from Chicago."

Lia shrugged again. "But that's life. Right? We had a cozy Christmas together, even if the place was a mess and we were going through Aunt Grace's things to donate. If you remember, we took Belle to the airport early on Christmas Eve so she could spend the holiday with her dad in Seattle."

"Exactly my point," Zach said. "It was chaotic. We had very little time together. I was looking forward to being alone with you this Christmas in our finally finished home here at the inn."

Maybe she saw his point. "Gosh, I am sorry. But I didn't think you would mind, and yes, I *should* have discussed it with you first. I did think about us, though—about how nice it would be to have some holiday festivities going on around us." She turned toward him, her voice inching up an octave with excitement. "I was thinking...."

"Oh no. I see that twinkle in your eye."

She grinned. "We could host a couple of community events, if you wanted, in the multipurpose room. It would be fun! Maybe a cookie exchange or a Secret Santa party for the kids in the area? What do you think?"

Zach exhaled. "I think it's two weeks until Christmas and that's not enough planning time."

Laughing, Lia waved her hand. "Oh pooh. Belle will help me organize and so will Alice. She can get the town on board, since she works for the mayor. And Julia loves to bake so she can help, too."

"And she's living with Sam now, so she's close."

"See? No problem. We can whip the holiday festivities into shape in no time."

Closing his eyes, Zach shook his head.

Lia smiled into her laptop. *Is my grumpy husband coming around?*

"We can have a private get together for our friends on Christmas day," she added. "I'll make a traditional Christmas dinner—oh! And you could invite some of your friends from town. I still haven't met a lot of their families, you know."

Zach eyed her. "I'm not sure my fishing buddies and your dysfunctional college girlfriends are a fit, to be honest. Besides, they all have families."

"Of course." Lia frowned. *My dysfunctional college girlfriends. Well, that's an exact description.* She couldn't deny that.

"So, to reiterate. You invited them all?"

"Well, yes—but it's just Maggie, Alice, and Julia. Wren and Willow are still AWOL. I sent out a group text message, hoping that maybe they would see it and respond, but—"

"But you know they will not show up, Lia. For whatever reason, those women have gone underground."

"I can always hope."

"Sure. It's been well over a year, though, and they're nowhere to be found."

"I get that. But there's a reason they disappeared, and I don't want to give up on them."

"So, your girlfriends are coming alone? Like the August beach week?"

Lia returned to her work, dodging his searching eyes, and studied the spreadsheet again. She tried to hide a frown but wasn't sure if Zach caught it. "Not sure. There will probably be kids."

"And significant others?"

"Maybe."

Zach stood. "This is getting bigger by the minute." He paused. "You realize half the rooms are shut down for deep cleaning and minor repairs. Right?"

Lia glanced back up. "Of course." He wasn't happy but was trying to hide it, she could tell. They rarely argued and tried to compromise when they didn't see things eye-to-eye, so her brain quickly raced over what the concession could be for this dilemma.

"I think I'm just going to dub this holiday Chaos Christmas."

"Oh geez, Zach. It will not be that bad!"

He peered at her. "Your friends are, at times, let me remind you, nothing less than a shit show."

Lia blew out a long breath. "Well, I know that, but look at Julia and

Sam. They are doing great. I'm not sure I can say the same for Alice or for Maggie."

"You think Maggie will actually come? How the hell will she get out from under Max's thumb? And you think Max will let those kids out of his sight over the holidays?"

"I know. She's had a rough couple of years with him, but I just talked with her. He's gone to Australia for the month of December. Queensland, I think she said. Business trip. Something to do with a big Australian Rodeo event."

"And he's not taking Maggie and the kids? It's Christmas!"

"No. In fact, he told Maggie to take the kids and come here to the beach."

"Well, I'm having a hard time believing that."

"It's what she told me." Lia knew too, that given what they had seen between Max and Maggie the summer before last—namely Max's control and emotional abuse over Maggie, and yes, sometimes physical abuse. It worried all of them. "Besides, she's safer here with us. I'm glad he's gone for a while."

"Me too. I don't like that man."

Lia looked back at the numbers on her spreadsheet, not really understanding any of them. "It will be fine, Zach. You'll see."

"What about Belle?"

"What *about* Belle?"

"Is she going to Seattle again?

"No! While the doctor said she could travel, she doesn't want to risk it, and I agree with that. That's a very long cross-country trip for anyone. Grant was a little miffed she wasn't coming, but he'll come around eventually when he realizes why."

"So, she hasn't told him about the baby."

"Apparently not. I wish she would, but I'm not interfering. That's her decision."

Zach cleared his throat. "I see. So, she will be here, too."

Lia glanced up, caught Zach's thin-lipped demeanor, and frowned. "What does that mean? She's my daughter! She's always going to be around."

He leaned over the desk. "Lia, I didn't mean it like that. I love Belle

with all my heart and always want her around. I'm just mentally calcu-
lating how many people could be here."

"Zach..." She stood, rounded her desk, and faced her husband.
Slowly, she snaked her arms around his waist. "You know Belle is going
through a bit of a rough time right now."

"I understand that. Maybe she doesn't want a bunch of people
around."

"And maybe she would like some company. You know, a distraction.
It could be good for her. Hey, maybe we can start a new tradition—
Christmas beach week!"

"Oh no. That's where I draw the line, Lia. We're not adding another
friendiversary beach week to the calendar. Let's take this holiday thing
one year at a time. Got that?"

He gathered her into his arms and kissed the tip of her nose.

"Got it." Lia smiled. "How about this tradeoff? The New Year
holiday is for us. New beginnings and all that. I'll make sure the girls
and their kids are gone a few days after Christmas. Can you tolerate
that? I told them to come by the 23rd, the day before Christmas Eve."

"It's not that I have to tolerate. I like your friends. I just wanted to
be alone with you this year—but all right, that's not happening, so we
go with the flow."

"With a ho, ho, ho!" Lia grinned.

Zach rolled his eyes. "Don't push it."

They both laughed.

LATER THAT AFTERNOON, BELLE GLANCED ACROSS THE
office at her mother, who was chatting on a four-way call with Maggie,
Alice, and Julia. Lia snorted with laughter at something someone said.

Belle wasn't paying much attention to their conversation, only that
they were obviously thrilled about the upcoming Christmas plans at Sea
Glass Inn.

She was excited about it in some ways, too. But dreaded it in others.

It was fun to think about everyone coming together at a different
time of the year. And she was looking forward to seeing her mother's

festive ideas come to fruition, too—plus she looked forward to helping.

On the other hand, this would be her last Christmas with her mother as a child—not that age twenty was still a child—because after this year, her Christmases would be spent with a child of her own.

Things were changing.

Am I ready for this?

Well, that was life. Right? While she was half scared out of her wits about the future—most of the time worried if she could actually do it—she was anxious, but also excited, about becoming a mother. It came earlier than she had expected—motherhood was something she'd always assumed would happen after she'd graduated from college and married.

But life, perhaps the universe, had other ideas. She'd made a choice that had altered her life and plans—but after a few months of living with reality, she was learning to accept the consequences of that momentary lapse of judgement.

Honestly? She was curious about the future.

She hoped she would be a good mother—but what if she wasn't?

Could she handle the chaos and the demands of motherhood? Could she afford to raise a child on her own in this day and age? Kids were expensive!

While she knew her mom and Zach and most likely her dad, too, would help, she didn't want to be a burden. She had to pull her weight.

She'd had outstanding role models with her own parents. The expectations were high.

Would she have a boy or a girl? She hadn't wanted to know the sex. Jenn called her old-fashioned, but she'd wanted to be surprised. None of those gender-reveal parties for her—she was keeping things low key, anyway.

Would she be a pool mom like her mother? Traipsing all over the state and beyond for swim meets? Up early every morning to drive to the pool for practice? That would be fun.

Or maybe she'd be a ball mom—like soccer or baseball or something. Perhaps her child would love horses or piano? The important thing, she would be one of *those* moms, wouldn't she? Encouraging her child and supporting them along the way.

Right. Good gracious. What her parents had done for her.

But there would be hard times, too. She was single and on her own.

Her dad had been around to help until she was nearly ten years old. And even after that, after he moved to Seattle, he had supported her financially. She wouldn't have the same support from her baby's father.

Not that she didn't have her mom and Zach to lean on—she did. The apartment they shared was spacious enough for the addition of a baby, but Belle knew in time she would want a place of her own. How would she swing that on her salary?

Zach had suggested carving out an apartment for the two of them— her and the baby—when the time came. They'd done that for Aunt Grace. Zach had added on rooms from the inn when she and her mom moved in. But that meant they would losing another suite or two, and that was income she didn't want them to sacrifice.

She had to find her own place. She had to stay in school, get her degree, and find a job.

She had to figure out life *with* a child, and *without* a partner.

While that pained her in some respects, it also relieved her in others —whatever decisions she had to make about her life and her child, were her decisions alone. She didn't have to think about anyone else. That was a comfort.

While her baby's father was cute and overpoweringly sexy, though a tad annoying and cocky—characteristics that had obviously drawn her to him last summer, for some odd reason—he wasn't father material.

She knew that now. He'd had his fun for the weekend, talked a good game, and promised he'd call her the next night, but didn't. His sister couldn't get off the phone fast enough when she'd had asked to speak to Chad, inquiring how she could get in touch with him.

In fact, Lucy Cooper didn't stay on the phone long enough for Belle to say who she was or what she wanted. It was almost like she'd had similar conversations prior to hers.

That's when she figured out that Chad was likely a player. And players don't make good partners—or fathers.

And that is that.

"Belle? Honey? What do you think?"

Her head jerked as her mother called out from across the room. "Excuse me?"

Lia rolled her eyes. "Goodness, sweetheart. I've been trying to get your attention. You're lost in a daydream, girl."

"Just thinking about some things. The baby...and classes." The last thing she wanted right now was to discuss what she'd been pondering. Time to divert. "Oh, and I've got an exam coming up. I am not ready for it. I should study."

"Then study!"

"I will later. I want to finish these reservation confirmations first."

Nodding, Lia shuffled a few things on her desk. "So, everyone is coming for the Christmas weekend. I'll need your help getting ready for the cookie exchange and the Santa thing. The girls are all excited." Looking up, she grinned at Belle.

"I heard Mom. I'm in the room, right? Your conference call...."

"Oh, right. I just get absorbed in the conversation."

And honestly, I have learned to tune your girlfriend calls out, so.... "What can I help with?"

"Are you sure you have time? Your classes and everything?"

With a sigh, Belle met her mother's gaze. "Of course, I have time. My last exam is tomorrow. Then I'm free."

"And you feel like helping? It might boost your spirits."

"Good gracious, Mom. I'm fine!"

"Oh, all right, then." Lia gathered up a notebook and some papers she'd doodled on earlier and headed to Belle's desk. "Here are some ideas I've been tossing about, and some tasks to be done, and I was wondering...." She plopped the papers down on Belle's desk and pulled up a chair. "Let's just go through this list and see what interests you. Okay?"

"That's perfect, Mom. I'm excited. This will be fun."

Lia's smile widened as she grasped Belle's hand and squeezed. "Good. Let's make this sparkle!"

Four

DECEMBER 23

BELLE WATCHED FROM THE FAR CORNER OF THE
multipurpose room as her mother and Zach chatted with friends and
townsfolk setting up for the festivities. Her mother had worked dili-
gently the past two weeks, scheduling and baking and decorating. She'd
created the plan, organized the events, called the people, and worked
with the local government through Alice to spread the word. Zach had
done his part, too, dragging holiday decorations out of storage, and
getting the room set up with tables and chairs.

Of course, she had also contributed to the cause, herself—calling
businesses all over town for donations of presents and cash, so everyone
who came left with something in their hands. She'd wrapped gifts and
bagged cookies and candy, making everything as festive as possible, and
had enjoyed her tasks. She had to admit, it helped her forget a few things
for a while.

Most of all, her working on the events had helped boost her holiday
mood.

A little.

Now, this afternoon late, she was glad to see a good crowd of people showing up for the First Annual Tuckaway Bay Christmas Cookie Exchange and Secret Santa Extravaganza—a mouthful to say the least—but that was what they had landed on to put on all the posters and flyers they'd shared around town.

Turning, she watched her mother stretch up on her tiptoes to plant a quick kiss on Zach's lips. The way they were together—her mother and her stepfather—made her smile. She could only hope for a similar relationship one day.

One day—if she stumbled upon a potential partner who was okay with a ready-made family.

Her mother had taken to beach-living so easily. Of course, she was head-over-heels in love with Zach and that made it easier for her to adjust. While Lia had put city life and Chicago behind her, Belle was still working on that. She loved the beach, and absolutely adored working with her mom running the inn, but she was becoming a bit of a loner, and that worried her.

Moreso, lately.

One might think it was easy to get lost in a small town, but the opposite was true—in a small town, you stand out. Everyone knows who you are.

And knows your business.

Right now, Belle wasn't interested in anyone in Tuckaway Bay knowing her business.

In Chicago, she would have easily blended into the population and life would have simply gone on. Life in Tuckaway Bay was like living in a fishbowl, always on display.

Maybe that would change come spring, when the tourists started infiltrating the area again.

"Belle? Honey?" Her mother called out. "Can you help me with these cookie trays?"

Glancing up, she saw her mother beckoning and waved back. "Of course."

THE DAY BEFORE CHRISTMAS EVE, AND THE OFFICIAL DAY OF the festivities, Lia's insides twittered with nervous energy. Not only were the events about to begin, but her friends were on their way to the beach!

The excitement was almost too much.

Moving through the multipurpose room, the scent of fresh pine and cinnamon mingled in the air as she made mental notes to add a few last-minute touches to the holiday décor. Who could resist more ribbons and garlands, tinsel and holly?

Rows of tables were decorated for the cookie exchange—and while the event didn't start for a couple of hours, early bakers had wandered in to stake their table claims. The massive Christmas tree stood in front of the windows—the rolling Atlantic in the background—ready to receive the Secret Santa gifts. The late December sun slanted into the room, casting a golden glow over the entire scenario—the perfect addition to her festive mood.

She hated to admit that the two weeks sped by ridiculously fast—and that perhaps Zach was right that it was a lot to plan for—but when they combined the cookie exchange with the secret Santa event, things came together quickly.

If she could only get her grumpy husband into the holiday spirit.

"Can you believe it's been a year since we've been here together?" Lia straightened a handcrafted sand dollar ornament on the tree, then glanced his way. "You know, I'm going to call you Scrooge if you don't wipe that silly frown off your face, Zachary Allen. Please get some holiday spunk about you before the children arrive!"

"Not frowning. Just intent on getting some things done."

"Frowning is what it looks like to me!"

Zach leaned against the doorway, an affectionate smile breaking over his lips. "All right, Mrs. Christmas. The frown is gone."

"That's better." Lia grinned and blew him a kiss. "Oh, and you confirmed with Jed Miller, right? We can't have a gift exchange without a Santa."

"He'll be here at five," Zach said, "...with bells on."

"And a red suit, I hope?"

He shrugged. "What else would he wear?"

"Well, since you frequently call him Jeb the Jokester, I'm not sure."

"Let's just call him Jeb the Jolly Old Elf today."

Rolling her eyes, she swatted at him. "That was lame, Zach."

He guffawed and stared out the window. "Those waves are really rolling. I should check the weather."

Lia followed his gaze. "I was thinking about that, too.

"It has been quite the journey, hasn't it?" he said after a moment. "While I'm still put off we're not spending the week alone, you were right to invite your friends. Plus, it's great what you are doing for the community, and I appreciate that."

"It's my community now, too." Lia grinned. "I want to celebrate the year we've had, and I can think of no better way. Everyone has been so supportive of our new venture." She moved a box from the floor to the table and pulled out a length of garland. "Plus, this is giving me ideas for next year."

She grinned and winked again.

Zach playfully rolled his eyes. "And next year is going to be fun with a little one running around, Granny Lia."

Twisting around quickly, Lia gasped. "Oh goodness. You are right!" A smile broke across her face. "Are you ready for that, Grandpa Z?"

Lia thought she saw a faint mist of tears in his eyes.

"I never thought I'd be a grandfather. Lia, you've brought so much into my life."

"And you've given all you have freely, Zach. We were meant for each other. You know?"

"I do know. I'm thankful."

"Me too, honey." Lia pulled a long strand of garland from the box. "Can you help me with this?"

"Why do you think I went after this ladder?"

"Well, you *are* the maintenance man."

"And the restaurant manager."

"And the substitute bartender."

He winked. "Only in the summer."

"True."

Zach hoisted the ladder to hang the garland above the sea-facing windows. Lia supervised, handing him fabric poinsettia flowers to place at strategic points. He glanced at the tree. "Need a hand with the star?"

"Oh yes. I nearly forgot." Lia handed it up and Zach secured the crowning piece atop the tree.

"Got it," he said with a chuckle. "There. Now it feels like Christmas."

"Wait till you taste the cookies I made for the exchange," she teased. "I tried out that recipe from Aunt Grace's old cookbook—you know, the one we found in that box in the hall closet?"

"The box full of postcards and letters and her journals?"

"Yes! Remember, she had hand-written recipe cards taped into a notebook."

"That's right. Maybe this winter we can go through that box."

"In the meantime, we have her cookies!"

"Should I be scared or excited?" Zach quipped, stepping down from the ladder and wrapping an arm around her shoulders.

"Definitely excited." Her laughter echoed softly through the room, adding to the symphony of holiday cheer. "They are crisp around the edges, chewy in the middle, and oh-so-very sweet!"

"As long as they don't have candied fruit in them, I'm fine. I'm not sure why Grace had this thing for candied fruit."

Lia snorted. "No candied fruit!"

They took a moment, side by side, to survey their handiwork—the twinkling lights, the lush greenery, the cozy nooks waiting to cradle their friends in comfort. Sea Glass Inn was more than a business—it was their home. It was a testament to their shared dreams, and a beacon of kinship on their own personal spot of the Outer Banks.

"I miss her," Zach said. "She would have loved this."

"Me too." Lia looked up into her husband's eyes.

His gaze drifted out the window and over the ocean.

"She's here in spirit."

"And she would love what you've done here." Zach turned back. "This place looks amazing. You have done an awesome job."

She leaned into him, her heart swelling with gratitude not only for their success but for the man beside her who made every challenge worth facing. "We make a pretty great team, don't we?"

"The best," he affirmed, planting a kiss on her temple. "Now, let's get ready to welcome friends, family, and community."

"I'm glad you're coming around."

"I'm working on it."

Lia raised up on her tiptoes to plant a soft kiss on Zach's lips. She lingered for a moment, nibbling, then drew back with a sigh.

"Perfect," he said, tugging her back into his arms. "Let's put on some holiday music to set the mood for a proper welcome."

"Sounds like a plan, Mr. Allen." Her heart thrummed with excitement. Her hopes for this weekend were coming to fruition. This Christmas, Sea Glass Inn was more than a vacation getaway—it was home, family, and friends—and perhaps the start of some new traditions. "I'm excited."

"Alright. Let's do this," Zach said.

"Absolutely."

"Hey Zach!" The voice came from across the room. Lia glanced that way and saw Melissa, their kitchen manager, standing by the entry with a platter full of chocolate cookies. "Can we pick any table for the exchange?"

"Pick a table, any table..." Zach said, nodding. With a quick peck on Lia's cheek, he added, "See you later. I need to check in with the restaurant." He headed toward Melissa.

"Hey!" Lia shouted.

Zach turned. "What?"

"You forgot something." She took two steps, leaned up on her tiptoes, and gave Zach a peck on the lips. "Also, don't forget to take the ladder back to storage. I don't want kids climbing on it."

He grinned and snapped his fingers. "Gotcha. Give me two minutes." Then he was off.

With a sigh, Lia moved into the kitchenette area of the multipurpose room and pulled two trays of cookies—Aunt Grace's Holiday Snickerdoodles—from underneath the counter. She nodded to Maisy Parker, a woman she'd met from a book club meeting she'd recently attended with Alice, who was carefully arranging her cookie creations on a table near the kitchenette.

"Those look yummy," Maisy called out. "I'm for sure going to exchange a few with you!"

"Oh, that's great." Lia glanced over at Maisy's table. "What have you got there?"

"Fruit cake bars!"

Lia laughed. "Oh, Zach will definitely love those!"

Maisy beamed.

Lia turned away to hide her smirky grin. Belle caught her eye from across the room. She watched her daughter for a few seconds, a little concerned about her deadpan expression, then waved and called out.

"Belle? Honey? Can you help me with these cookie trays?"

Belle waved back and nodded. "Of course, Mom."

"Thanks, sweetie. There are more under the counter. And some more Christmas platters, too."

Pretending to organize the red, green, and white sugary confections on a Christmas tree platter, Lia moved them around a bit while watching her daughter. Belle's gaze was downcast, avoiding eye contact with others in the room, until she approached the kitchenette counter and looked up.

Her weak smile hit with an uneasy thud in Lia's stomach. Her girl was either unhappy, or not well, and that was worrisome.

"You okay, honey?"

Belle sighed. "Just a little tired, is all."

Lia nodded. She supposed that was to be expected.

Five

Her phone vibrated on her hip a couple of hours later. Lia knew the chime alone wouldn't cut through the noisy and festive Christmas cookie shenanigans and wanted to make sure she didn't miss a call or text from one of her girlfriends. More people than she had expected showed up for the cookie exchange, and the multipurpose room teamed with activity. Zach made sure the Christmas music playlist he'd created played on a continuous loop.

She fished her phone from her back jeans pocket, her heart skipping a beat.

"Here we go," she breathed. Glancing at Zach, she swiped the screen. "It's Maggie. The Christmas chaos begins!"

He groaned.

Maggie: *Roads clear. Light traffic. Carol's playlist is tolerable. LOL*

Maggie: *Making good time. Be there in an hour. XO Mags.*

Lia: *Can't wait!*

"She's an hour out." A surge of joy bubbled up within her. It had been several months since she'd seen Maggie—since beach week last August—and that hadn't ended well. She showed Zach the message.

"So, it's a definite Carol is coming."

"Yes." Lia shrugged. "And the little kids."

"How many does she have again?"

"Three."

"Three plus Carol?"

"No, three including Carol."

He whistled out a breath. "Goodness. And how many other kids?"

"Just Ella, you know, Alice and George's daughter." Lia registered the anxious look on Zach's face. "It's Christmas! You expect the mothers to abandon their children during the Christmas holiday?"

"Well, no. But what about their spouses?"

Lia sneered. "That's a different story."

"And one I don't want to hear right now."

"Probably not."

A notification popped up on Lia's phone again. She glanced down. Zach read the message over her shoulder.

Alice: *Ella and I are packing.*

Alice lived across town, on the opposite side of Tuckaway Bay, the sound side of the island. Lia knew once she started out, it would only take her about twenty minutes to drive over.

Lia: *Great! George too?*

A few silent seconds ticked by, then....

Alice: *No. He's going to the cabin.*

Lia knew George's family had a cabin up in the Blue Ridge mountains. Frowning, she looked up at Zach. He shrugged.

Lia: *Oh?*

Alice: *Talk later.*

Hmm.

A few more seconds passed.

Julia: *Sam and I are on our way. Picked up Hannah in Norfolk.*

"Hannah?" Zach asked.

"Sam's daughter."

"Another kid? And who knew Sam had a daughter?"

Lia sighed. "I did because Julia told me. And she's not a kid, she's like twenty-one or something. Near Belle's age."

"And she's staying here too?"

"Well, Sam and Julia are staying at Gull Cottage, for old times' sake. I guess she'll stay with them."

Zach closed his eyes. "I thought they'd stay at Sam's house and pop in occasionally."

Lia angled her gaze and gave him a sassy smile. "Now, what kind of fun would that be? I need all my people in one place."

Zach inwardly groaned, but Lia could hear it. She waved him off. "Oh, another text."

Julia: *That okay? That Hannah's here?*

Lia: *Of course! Drive safe.*

Julia: *Will do.*

The chat fell silent. No word, of course, from Wren or Willow. That was the only thing that made Lia's heart heavy this holiday season. The last time they heard from the sisters was a picture sent via the group text —a picture of Willow holding a newborn baby.

At least the others thought it was Willow. Lia wasn't so sure. It could have been Wren. The identical twins were so much alike that pictures were always difficult.

She hoped that wherever they were, they were safe and happy.

The next hour flew by—the cookie bakers exchanged their confections and recipes, filling their baskets and bins to the brim with goodies. As five o'clock approached, Lia noticed the Christmas tree was full of gifts—in fact, overflowing.

Jeb arrived on cue, barreling into the room with a loud, "Ho ho ho!" The children erupted with laughter and raced toward him.

As he started passing out the Secret Santa gifts, the door to the multipurpose room flew open and in stumbled Maggie and her children, Carol, Jason, and Chloe.

"Maggie!" Lia waved.

The younger kids ran wide-eyed toward Santa. Lia was suddenly glad she'd put special gifts under the tree for all her friends' children. Carol managed a half-hearted *"I'm bored already"* eye roll and hung back, picking at her manicure.

"Lia!" Maggie jumped up and down, her hands fluttering, then glanced behind her. Alice and Ella popped into the room.

They spotted Lia and waved.

"Alice! Ella!" She headed across the room, giddiness welling up inside her.

Just as she reached to hug Maggie, the door swung open again. Julia, Sam, and a young woman, apparently Hannah, stepped inside.

"Oh, my God." Maggie exclaimed. "You all look great!"

"Just glad we are all here," Alice said. "Well, except for... You know."

Yeah, they all knew. The AWOL twins.

Lia hugged Maggie. "I see Alice and Julia all the time now. Seems like forever since I've seen you."

"It was just August, but I know what you mean."

Julia interrupted. "Ladies, quick intro here. This is Hannah, Sam's daughter."

Hannah nodded and smiled. "Hi. Thanks for having me. First time this far east."

"And you're about as east as you can get!" Alice touched Hannah's arm. "So glad to meet you. I'm Alice, and this is my daughter, Ella."

Ella grinned.

Hannah nodded.

"And I'm Maggie." She tossed a little wave and then tugged at Carol's shirt sleeve. "This is Carol, my oldest, and my other two are over there somewhere under the tree."

Hannah's head kept bobbing.

"Hey," Carol mumbled.

"I'm Lia, Hannah." Lia pushed out her hand and Hannah shook it. "Good gracious, Sam. You've been holding out on us. She's lovely."

Hannah's cheeks pinked a little.

Sam gave Lia an awkward look, so she hurried on. "We're happy to have you here at Sea Glass Inn, Hannah. My husband, Zach, and I own the place. Our daughter Belle is around here somewhere—I'll introduce you two later. Welcome!"

"It's...beachy." She glanced around. "And I'm..." She turned to Sam. "Yeah. I guess I belong to him." She laughed nervously.

Sam's expression was unreadable.

Julia looked a little uncomfortable.

Lia couldn't blame Hannah for being nervous, though. Or for Sam and Julia to feel uncertain. She knew from Julia that Hannah's visit was a test, of sorts. Plus, this crew was a lot to handle.

After a few more minutes of chatting, hugging, and squealing, Zach moved into the group. "Welcome to Sea Glass Inn!" he said. "Or as I'm dubbing it for the weekend, Christmas Chaos. Do you all want to get settled into your rooms now or later?"

Lia knew he was forcing the smile, and she loved him for it. She also knew his joke was half-way serious.

"Thanks, Zach. Nice to be here. Appreciate the invite." Sam pushed out his hand.

Zach shook it. "Now I'm not absolutely certain, Sam Watters, but I don't think I've ever seen you before without your fishing hat."

"Or a pole in his hands?" Julia laughed.

"Right."

"Oh Zach," Maggie interjected. "If you don't mind, I'd love to check into our room. I need a tiny break from driving and the kids do, too." She motioned for Jason and Chloe. "But we will be back soon for all the fun."

"Works for me, too," Alice added.

"Same," said Julia, "but all we need is the key. We know the way."

"Perfect." Zach nodded. "The keys are in the office next door. Let's head over."

They all exited into the hallway and Zach half leaned toward Lia's ear and whispered. "Hail, hail, the gang's all here."

Lia laughed. "So, let it snow, let it snow, let it snow?"

"Bite your tongue, woman. It may turn out to be more like blow, blow, blow. Looks like stormy weather ahead."

Stormy weather? Inside or outside the inn?

Lia shook off the ambiguity and watched Zach point the way to the office. Then turning on her heel, she scurried off toward the Secret Santa frivolity, refusing to let a few silly words put a damper on the holiday.

BELLE HAD TO ADMIT THAT WATCHING THE CHILDREN OPEN their gifts from their Secret Santa, their eyes wide with excitement when Santa called their names and they approached the jolly old elf, made her heart full and happy.

For a while, she forgot all about her situation and simply enjoyed the moment.

"Having fun?" Her mother stepped up beside her. "Those kids' reactions are purely precious."

Belle nodded. "Kinda magical. Hearing them laugh makes me want to laugh too."

"Christmas is magical!"

She could almost feel her mother's stare on the side of her face.

"It's good to hear you laugh, too, sweetheart."

Slowly, she faced her mother. "I know. I've been a Moody Milly the past few months."

"Part of that is hormones," her mother said, "but you also seem a bit down."

Belle tugged on her lower lip with her teeth and bit it.

"When you do that, I know you are worried."

The last thing she wanted to do was worry her mother. Reaching out, she gave her a hug. "You're too perceptive. I've just been thinking about being a mother. Mom, I'm not sure I can do it. How did you do everything you did when I was little? You worked and everything."

"And went to graduate school."

"I'm not sure I have the discipline."

Her mother glared. "Belle! You're the most disciplined child I've ever known. Do you realize what it takes to do what you did day after day when you were swimming competitively?"

"But that's because you were there to push me. I'm not sure I can do that."

"Push you? Goodness. You were the one pushing me out of bed at o-dark-thirty to get your breakfast and get on the road. Don't you remember?"

"But raising a child is not only about swim practice."

"No, it's not. But if there is one thing I know about you, darling, you know how to figure it out. And you'll figure out the right way for you to be a mom. Besides," she paused, brushing a few stray hairs from Belle's face, "it's more of a one day at a time thing, and you've got a lot of days ahead. Plus, you're not alone."

"I know."

Lia smiled. "Cheer up. It's Christmas!"

Belle grinned. "I'm fine. Watching the children has helped."

Lia draped an arm around Belle's shoulder, then gazed over the roomful of kids. "Oh, sweetie. Next Christmas we'll have a little one here, too."

Belle sucked in a breath. "You're going to be a grandmother."

Leaning in, her mother whispered, "But a young sexy grandma, according to Zach."

"I don't need to know that!"

Lia grinned and trotted off, playing host and talking with people as she made her way through the room.

Belle sighed. Her mother was something else.

There *was* something about the magic of Christmas, though, that she'd always loved, and honestly, looked forward to sharing with her child—she'd never imagined doing it alone.

That was part of her melancholy, wasn't it? She was alone.

She'd always expected she'd share the holidays with a husband.

"Note to Belle," she whispered to herself. "Get over it."

A COUPLE OF HOURS LATER, THE COOKIE EXCHANGERS gathered their hauls, merrily chatting all the while, and headed toward the exit. Jeb, aka Santa, made his rounds, helping clean up the area around the Christmas tree where children had tossed wrapping paper and ribbons when opening their gifts. Her mother and Zach stood at the door, thanking everyone for coming, and wishing them all happy holidays as they left.

Sam's daughter strolled toward her.

"Wow, some party, huh?" she said. "I'm Hannah, by the way. And you're Belle? Did you help with all of this?"

"Yes, I'm Belle." She grinned. Might be nice having someone her age around, and she liked Hannah's smile. "I did some things. Mom and Zach did the most work."

"Well, it was quite the event. I'm impressed."

Belle turned toward Hannah. "Thanks. It's the kind of thing we do around here."

Grinning, Hannah nudged her arm. "So, is there an after party? Like, for young adults and hopefully one that includes inappropriate adult beverages?"

Belle laughed. "I wish. It's been a minute since I've been inappropriate."

"Ha! Well, I had to ask."

"Most every place around here is closed for the season—bars and restaurants, specifically over the holiday weekend. I think we're pretty much stuck here for the night, especially with the storm coming in."

She shrugged. "I'm okay with that. The little kids are watching Home Alone on the TV in the corner. I'm always up for a good Christmas comedy. Want to join me?"

"Sure. I'll find some snacks. Maybe hot chocolate?"

"Got any whiskey for that?"

"Hmm." Belle grinned. "Perhaps. Let me see what I can dig up."

"I would love you forever."

"Great. See you in a few. Oh, and maybe grab Carol and Ella."

Glancing about, Hannah nodded. "Perfect. I see them over by the tree."

"Meet you there."

Belle watched Hannah saunter off. They'd just met, of course, so she wasn't sure about her, but she seemed nice enough. She joined the little kids watching the movie on the oversized television screen Zach had mounted there last summer. He'd also installed glass garage doors, opening up the entire backside of the room to the patio and beach. Those, of course, were closed tonight—but in the summer, they would be wide open for movie nights around the pool.

She smiled. Zach and her mom were always thinking about the guests, making sure they had a good experience while staying at Sea Glass Inn.

With a sigh, she cracked a quick smile. Her child could do a lot worse in life, right?

Six

"There you all are."

Lia made her way to the pool-side deck behind Sea Glass Inn. The sun had nearly set over the sound, shooting trails of orange and pink across the silver-blue sky, while the Atlantic churned toward the shore in the opposite direction, dusting her cheeks with a salty mist.

The evening air held a slight chill—of course, it *was* December—but the hotel protected them from the nippy breeze. Actually, the spot was quite cozy. Lia kept stacks of soft cushions and thick blankets near the wooden beach chairs, and this time of year if there were guests, Zach made sure there was a crackling fire in the fire pit.

Julia, Maggie, and Alice were already there, chatting softly.

"I wondered where you all had wandered off to," Lia said warmly. She plopped down into a chair on Julia's left. "Whew. All over but the final cleanup. I'll do that tomorrow."

"We'll help," Maggie said.

"Yes. What a great job, Lia." Alice smiled. "The kids loved it."

"Amen to that." Julia drew her blanket around her shoulders. "What's everyone doing inside?"

Lia gave a sigh. "Well, Zach's off showing Sam his new fishing gear, the little kids are watching a movie, and the older girls are keeping an eye on them. Sounds like they are getting to know each other."

"Oh, that's great," Maggie said. "Carol could use some influence by some older, more mature young ladies."

Lia let that sink in, but wasn't about to respond. "They looked to be deep into discussion."

"Interesting." Maggie sat back. "They are all close in age, aren't they?"

"Within a few years, I would guess. Belle just turned twenty," Lia said.

"Hannah is twenty-one," Julia added.

Alice shifted in her seat. "Ella turned eighteen last month."

"And Carol had birthday number seventeen in June," Maggie offered. "A difficult seventeen, I might add."

"Good gracious." Alice sighed. "They all have their moments, Mags. I guess we did too."

"I suppose."

"Gosh," Julia said. "Do you all realize they are all practically the same age we were when we first met?"

Alice leaned forward. "You're right! I remember that day our freshman year like it was yesterday."

"We really were lucky that the university paired us up like they did. If they hadn't, we never would have met."

Lia laughed. "Gosh, I remember that day so well. I arrived late, and the three of you had already moved into the dorm suite. I took one teeny bitty glance and knew we were going to be best friends for life."

"Are you sure about that, Lia?" Maggie scoffed. "You were sort of sweet and innocent when you arrived. I think Julia and I may have corrupted you somewhat."

Julia coughed. "Um, no. That was all you, Mags."

"Oh, never to worry. I kept everyone in line."

"That you did, Mother Hen Alice." Maggie smirked.

Lia adjusted her cushions and pulled her legs up under her, eager to shift the conversation. "Oh, you all! We were perfect—just perfect—for each other."

"And then when we moved in the twins—six women in that four-woman suite—all hell broke loose!" Julia laughed.

They all laughed too.

"Very true. But what fun times. Mostly."

For a moment, they all grew silent. Lia was sure they were all thinking about Wren and Willow. Yes, there were tons of good times—and also some that were not so great.

She wasn't ready to get into issues. *Not yet.* Time to switch gears. "Did you all have fun this evening?"

Alice quickly responded. "Lia, what you did for the community today was simply amazing. Marilyn hopes you're going to make it an annual event."

"Well, as long as the Mayor of Tuckaway Bay is pleased, I'm happy." Lia teased and Alice's cheeks flushed a little at the mention of Marilyn. They all knew she was in love with her boss—and George knew it, too —but the information was not for public consumption. "With more time to plan, it could happen, but I'll need to confer with the grumpy boss man."

The ladies laughed.

She glanced back at the hotel. "I asked Belle to bring us some hot chocolate. She should be here any minute."

"Oh, lovely."

"Perfect!"

"Yum!"

As if on cue, Belle exited the multipurpose room door to the pool patio, carrying a tray of steaming mugs. She sat the tray on a table next to her mother. "Here you go."

"Thanks, honey."

"Need anything else?" Belle asked. "I'm going back in. We're watching a movie."

Lia shook her head. "I think we're good. Did you get hot chocolate for all the kids?"

"Oh yes. Hot chocolate all around." Belle gave her mother a half-smile and left.

"Have fun, honey. Hang out with the girls."

Belle paused and glanced over her shoulder, tossing her mother a slight nod.

Julia inhaled deep over the steamy tray of chocolate. "She okay?"

Lia sighed. "She's coming to terms with things."

Reaching toward Lia, Alice patted her hand. "She'll be a great mother because she has you for a role model."

Smiling, Lia grasped Alice's hand. "Thanks."

"Wait. What?" Maggie sat straight up. "Belle is pregnant? Why didn't I know this?"

The other three women glared.

Lia blinked. "I'm not sure. I thought you knew."

"Well, I didn't. Oh, poor Belle. Goodness. Her life is going to change now. Is she going to keep it?"

Julia whipped her entire body around toward Maggie. "Good God, Maggie. Of course she is. Now just shut up about it."

Maggie opened her mouth to say something, glanced at the group, then closed her mouth again and sat back.

"I'm sorry. I thought I'd mentioned it." Lia met Maggie's gaze.

"Maybe I missed it."

"Maybe. You haven't been reading or responding to texts, you know." Lia surprised herself that she'd confronted Maggie with her lack of communication.

"When's the baby due?"

Lia sighed and silently wished for an Old Fashioned, although she knew she wouldn't drink in front of Julia. "She's about thirty-four weeks."

"Boy or girl?" Maggie inquired.

"She doesn't want to know yet."

Maggie cocked her head. "Wow. She sure doesn't look that far along. I thought she'd just gained a little bit of weight."

"She did gain some weight when she stopped swimming as much," Lia explained, "but overall, she's in really good shape, and she's all baby. She's watched her diet and walks too. Her baby bump has expanded the past couple of months, but she hides it well."

"Is she trying to hide the pregnancy?" Alice asked.

"Oh, no." Lia didn't want to give that impression. "She's private about it, but not hiding it. I didn't mean that. You know, maternity clothes are so different these days than when we were pregnant. Besides, she loves wearing Boho dresses and those baggy jumpsuit things. She just tries to be comfortable."

"Yeah," Maggie agreed. "Those loose dresses hide a multitude of sins." Her eyes shot wide then as she looked at Lia. "Not that what Belle did was a sin or anything. I didn't mean that. Of all people, I guess, I shouldn't even be talking about sin...."

Alice cleared her throat. "We get it, Maggie."

Lia worried about Julia, with the mention of babies and maternity clothes and all that, and glanced her way.

Julia reached for her hand. "Is Belle okay though, honey? This is a huge, unexpected life change. Is there anything we can do to help her—or you—through all of this?"

She felt Julia's compassion and sniffled. She would not cry, even though sometimes she felt like it. "I'm concerned, of course, because of her heart. And also, she seems a bit depressed, which also isn't good for her health."

Julia squeezed her hand harder.

Maggie sat straight up. "Oh, my God! I didn't think about her heart. Will delivering the baby be too much stress on her? Is this dangerous?"

Discussing this with her girlfriends was the last thing she wanted to do right now—Lia rarely placed attention on herself—but maybe she should talk a little. She closed her eyes briefly, blew out a breath, then glanced around the group. "It's scared the hell out of me, to be honest."

"Of course it has, honey!" Alice scooted her chair closer. "But we're here for you. And Belle. You know that. Right?"

"I do."

"What do the doctors say?"

Lia told them about their visit to Chicago with Ned Speakman in October, the tests and conference calls, and the delivery plans at the Outer Banks hospital. "They say everything is fine and they are expecting a normal delivery—but if needed, they are prepared to do a C-section. They have all of Belle's wishes written up in a plan, and her cardiology team at Chicago Med has approved everything."

"So in other words," Julia said, "All precautions have been taken and everything looks normal."

Lia nodded. "That's right."

"But it's still worrisome as fuck," Julia added.

"To put it bluntly, yes. But we are going to get through this and come next Christmas, I'll have a beautiful grandchild here with me." Lia smiled, although her heart was heavy just having this conversation.

Alice leaned closer. "We know you are scared, honey, but we are all here for you."

Lia glanced about again with misty eyes and smiled. "Thank you."

Julia twisted and leaned over the mugs of hot chocolate to her left. "Mmm, smells amazing. These are going to get cold soon if we don't drink them. Who wants a mug?"

Bless you, Julia, for this change of subject. "Help yourself, ladies. It's my special recipe."

Soon they cradled their mugs, the rich aroma filling the air. A contented silence edged with a tiny bit of tension, settled over the friends as they sipped. The popping fire provided a calming backdrop.

"I detect peppermint, lots of sugar, and something else..." Julia said.

"Besides chocolate?" Maggie grinned.

"Yes," Julia said, taking another taste. "Coffee. Is this a hot mocha with peppermint?"

Lia smiled. "Half dark chocolate, half white chocolate, sweetened condensed milk, coffee, and peppermint. Yes! And a secret ingredient I will not divulge."

"You are a bitch, Lia." Julia sneered, jokingly.

Everyone laughed again.

"Yummy," Maggie said, drawing her legs up into her wooden chair and covering them with a blanket. "I love it."

"Me too," Alice echoed.

"It's wonderful being back here," Maggie added, her eyes crinkling. "I want you all to know that. Tuckaway Bay is so special, so peaceful. It's just what I needed."

Lia nodded. "I'm glad, Maggie. Truly, I am.

After several silent seconds, Julia spoke up, her expression serious. "So... How is everyone? Really."

NO ONE SAID ANYTHING FOR SEVERAL MINUTES.

Lia exchanged glances with all three women. Their reunions were a chance to let their guard down, honestly, but would that happen tonight? Usually, they were alone—and there was alcohol—but tonight the circumstances were very different.

Maybe it was too soon to get into heavy discussions.

"Seriously," Julia said. "We can discuss another time. I was just curious."

Alice sighed heavily. "The divorce has been so much harder on Ella than we expected. She's become so withdrawn lately. And George? He's... Well. I can't explain it."

Leaning closer, Lia spoke softly. "So, you've told Ella? I wasn't sure."

Alice nodded. "Yes. She graduates in the spring and has been accepted at ECU, so she's making college plans. We weren't going to tell her until after she was settled there in the fall, but she overheard a conversation—well, a fight—and we had to explain."

"Oh shit," Julia hissed.

"Yeah."

"You and George fight?" Maggie raised a brow. "I honestly can't imagine that."

"Well, we do lately," Alice admitted.

"So, she now knows you're gay?" Maggie shifted in her chair. "I mean. A lesbian? Geez, Alice, what are you? A bisexual person, maybe? Does she know about you and the mayor? I mean, Marilyn?"

"I'm bi. And no, she doesn't know that. All she knows is that her father and I are divorcing."

"Are you still living in the same house?"

Alice nodded toward Julia. "Yes, because George wants to. He refuses to move until after she goes to college."

"Is that difficult for you?"

"No. I'm just... I'm just antsy. George, to be honest, is faltering. A couple of years ago, he was all for an amicable separation, but now he's acting weird about it. I feel like another shoe is about to drop and I don't know when, or why."

"Oh, honey..." Maggie reached out and grasped Alice's hand. "Believe me. I know how you feel. We need to find some time to talk."

Alice nodded.

"Speaking of…" Lia met Maggie's gaze. "What's the deal with Max going to Australia?"

"Forget that for a minute," Julia interjected, pitching her body forward. "I want to know about the cowboy. Whatever happened there?"

Maggie rolled her eyes and sighed. "He's long gone, and it's for the best. It was a fun run while it was happening, but to be honest, I'm glad he made the break. He had a girlfriend back home in Alabama, and I was simply his North Carolina diversion."

"Well, shit," Julia blurted out. "And you risked so much to be with him. Even though it was wrong, I'll add."

Shrugging, Maggie lowered her gaze, then tossed them a sassy grin. "But damn, the sex was *abso-fucking-delicious* while it lasted."

Giggles broke out over the group. "Maggie, you always make me laugh," Lia said. "I have to say, though, I'm glad the cowboy is history. So, about Australia…."

"I don't really know that much. Max keeps his business practices private. The only thing he talked about was an opportunity in Queensland to plan this massive rodeo event. Usually Max does golf tournaments, so he thinks this offers an opportunity for the growth of his event planning business. You know, branching out."

"Didn't he go to Australia a while back?"

Maggie nodded. "Yes, he hosted a big golf event then. I guess he made some new contacts, and they introduced him to other people. He's gone a few more times over the past year, and apparently has been working on this deal for a while."

"Hmm." Julia sat back.

"But a month? And at Christmas?" Alice rolled her eyes. "I would think he'd want to be with his family at Christmas."

Maggie shrugged again. "I know, but he said it was such a long trip, and that there were a lot of meetings, and he didn't want to fly back and forth—so he rented a short-term apartment and is staying the month, at least."

"And he couldn't take all of you." That was a firm statement from Julia.

Maggie quickly shook her head. "No, the kids. School. Holidays. You know. Besides, he'll be busy. He's wanting to close the deal this time and didn't want the distraction of kids."

Lia watched Julia smirk. "You said he'd be gone a month. At least?"

"That's what he said."

"I see." Julia raised a brow. "So, once he lands the deal, I assume that means he'll be making more trips to Queensland?"

"Well, yes."

"I see."

Lia watched Maggie's expression turn solemn as she stared at Julia. "Please don't make more of this than what it is. I'm sort of glad for the break from all men for a few weeks."

Nodding, Julia agreed. "I get that. Not judging and not thinking about Max. Only you, sweetie. You've been through enough shit."

"Thank you." Maggie smiled, pausing to study Julia. "And how are you, my friend?"

Inhaling deep, Julia let the breath flow out quickly. "Five months sober, so that's a celebration. My life has done a 180 with Sam and I couldn't be happier."

"And Sam?"

Julia beamed. "He's good too. We are good for each other."

"Well, that's great news for sure," Maggie added.

"Sam is such a nice guy," Lia shared. "He and Aunt Grace were friends for years. He is the only local person she let fish on her property. Zach highly respects him." She smiled at Julia. "And I am very happy for you."

"Thank you, Lia."

Lia hesitated, then blurted out. "Is Mark okay? You've not mentioned him lately, so I'm just curious." She knew Julia's ex-husband was running the bed-and-breakfast back in Louisville, but wondered how he was coping now that Julia had moved to Tuckaway Bay.

Julia sat back in her chair and pulled her feet up under the blanket. "Apparently, he is fine. He's recovering from the accident and the wheelchair is less of an issue now. His paralysis hasn't been the handicap he worried it would be. Oh, and he and Pam have set a wedding date."

"Wow!" Maggie leaned forward. "Are you okay with that?"

"I'm perfectly fine, Mags." She laughed. "I love Pam like a sister—she was so much help to me when I first started running the B&B by myself—and I know she will be good for Mark. Just the woman he needs, honestly."

"Well, that's really awesome," Maggie said. "Seems like you all are in a good place."

"We're working on it, I guess you would say. This visit with Hannah could be a bit of a stumbling block for all three of us, but that remains to be seen."

Alice stood and stretched, then placed her empty mug on the tray. "So, tell us about Hannah."

Julia sat back in her chair. "It's touchy between her and Sam, a long story for another day. He was absent so much from her life growing up and there is a certain level of bitterness, but now that she's older, they are trying to work on a relationship."

"And of course, now you're tossed in the mix. Right?" Lia asked. "Does that make it more challenging?"

"For sure. It's going to be an interesting week, I imagine. Although we got along fine over the short Thanksgiving holiday." Julia paused and studied Lia for a moment. "You recently had your first anniversary, right?"

"Yes. One year of marriage in the books. And one year of successfully running the resort. The inn is fantastic. Zach, of course, is great. But I have to confess, he wasn't too keen on us not having Christmas alone this year. I should have talked with him before I invited all of you but, he's getting over it."

"Oh?"

"If he's grumpy, that's why."

Alice sat up. "Oh, Lia. Should we leave?"

"Heck no! I want you here."

"Well," Julia said, "The least we can do, ladies, is promise Lia there will be no drama. Right?"

Maggie nodded. "No drama. Absolutely no drama. Cross my heart."

They all laughed.

Julia glanced at Alice. "Right?"

"Of course. This is a drama-free zone. No chaos allowed."

Julia smiled at Lia. "See? Everything will be fine.

Sure. Right. Awesome. "I love you guys." Glancing back to the inn, she saw Zach slip out the back door. "And speak of the handsome devil...."

"What? Hot chocolate?" Zach eyed the empty mugs. "Without Sam and me?"

"Ask Belle. I'm sure she made a pot full," Lia told him. "In the kitchen."

"Will do. Just wanted to tell you all to have fun this evening."

"Oh, we definitely are. This is so cozy, Zach. The perfect place for us to catch up on girl talk." Julia looked up at him. "Thanks for building the fire, too."

"No problem. Enjoy it while you can."

Maggie leaned forward. "Why? Something going on?"

Lia caught Maggie's nervous expression and wondered if she was as relaxed as she made out to be earlier.

"Well..." he started. "The weather is tanking off the coast. Big Nor'easter is taking a southerly dive within the next day. Might be the only night to enjoy the deck."

"Oh wow," Julia said. "That's a shame. Although, it could make for an interesting Christmas Eve tomorrow."

"And Christmas day," Zach added.

"Yeah." Maggie gathered her blanket up closer to her neck. "Maybe I'll sleep out here tonight. You know, with the waves in my ears, the breeze in my hair...."

Lia stood. "And what about your kids?"

Maggie laughed and swatted the air. "Kids? Oh, that's right. I have kids. I thought I was twenty again, unencumbered and carefree."

"Right." Lia laughed. "Just open your windows in your suite. You'll hear the waves for sure, and your kids will be safe."

Maggie closed her eyes. "I'd rather be out here, to be honest, dreaming about when we were twenty and drinking tequila and smoking weed...."

"And Wren and Willow were with us."

"Yes."

Alice sighed and leaned back. "Now, those were the days...."

Seven

CHRISTMAS EVE MORNING

IT WASN'T LIKE SHE NEEDED FRIENDS.

Hang out with the girls, her mother had said last night.

Quit pushing, Mom.

She really had nothing in common with the other girls. Carol was immature. Ella was still in high school. Hannah, apparently, was in graduate school. And she? Belle? College dropout, office worker, single, and pregnant.

No. The four of them would likely never be good friends.

Not like their moms, anyway.

She had friends in Tuckaway Bay. Jenn, of course, was her best girlfriend, and she was becoming closer friends with Melissa, the kitchen manager. She'd also made casual friends with some girls who worked at Seaside Shoppes Mall, which used to be her favorite place to shop. They would go out occasionally, to a movie, or shop, or get something to eat.

But she wouldn't be shopping with any of them anytime soon. They don't want to shop for maternity clothes or baby things, anyway. And after the baby? Well, she'd have a little human to take care of.

Life would never be the same.

With a sigh, she focused on the reservation software showing on her laptop. She'd been staring at it for some time, not really seeing anything. And while it was Christmas Eve, and they were expecting no new guests today, she needed to do something routine, which was why she was at her desk.

Reviewing the guest list—the check-ins and departures—was her first task every morning.

She forced herself to concentrate.

Scrolling over the day's events, she realized her task was easy.

No check-ins. No departures.

Twelve rooms and two suites were closed for cleaning and painting.

Alice and Maggie occupied two suites with their kids. Guests—one family, two couples, and one single man—had booked the other four units. One suite was empty. Two more rooms were available.

Four of the six cottages were also booked. Sam and Julia were staying in the Gull. A large family had rented the Tortoise Shell and the Pelican's Nest. The Loggerhead and Dolphin were closed. The Sandpiper was empty.

That meant they had one cottage, one suite, and two rooms available if they had last-minute calls or walk-ins. Which, she hoped, was unlikely on Christmas Eve.

Glancing up, she looked out the window next to her desk at the rough seas hitting the shore. "Especially in this weather," she said aloud.

"What's that?"

Belle twisted to see her mother walk in the office door. "Just mumbling about the weather. Looks a bit scary out there."

Lia paused, looking out at the ocean. "Yes. And to be honest, it worries me."

"It will be fine, Mom."

Smiling, Lia agreed. "Of course."

Storms here were nothing like what they got in Chicago. Living so close to the ocean, Belle knew her mother got nervous thinking about hurricanes and such. Zach was always good to ease her fears, but this storm—well, even Zach appeared somewhat concerned earlier that morning.

"Have you checked the weather report lately?"

Lia nodded. "The storm is gaining speed. They are predicting unusually gusty winds, heavy rainfall, and flooding. Tonight and tomorrow should be the worst of it."

"Goodness. On Christmas Day!"

"I know."

"Oh my gosh, Mom. Are we okay here?"

"Zach says we are. The hotel is high on pilings and sits back from the ocean. He is worried about Gull Cottage, because it's closer to the surf, especially during high tide and then, if there is flooding..." Lia paced a little, looking out the window and clutching her hands together. "He also said we need to board up the hotel windows on the ocean side. At least on the ocean level and first floor."

"Oh, wow. That sounds serious." Belle sighed and glanced again at her computer. "Maybe we should ask Sam and Julia to move into the hotel. We have one suite available."

"Yes." Lia rotated toward her desk, nodding. "Let's talk to them at breakfast. I don't want to panic anyone but...."

"You're already panicking, Mom."

Turning, Lia grinned. "You know me too well."

"Yep."

"I'm just glad you stayed here for the holidays, rather than go to Seattle. We would have been taking you to the airport this morning. I wonder if any flights will go out?"

"Probably not." Belle stood and joined her mother at the window. "Goodness, those waves are super high and rolling in with some speed."

"Let's not dwell on it." Lia turned away from the window and put her arm around Belle's shoulders. "But you should probably give your dad a call."

"I will. They are spending the day with Ginger's parents, I think, and will be home this evening. I'll call then."

"Good idea." Pausing, Lia glanced off. "Belle, I hate to push this, but you still haven't told him. Have you?"

Blinking twice, she faced her mom. "No. I had planned to before now, but I couldn't. I just need to find the right words."

"Soon, okay? He may need time to get used to the idea. You only have a few weeks."

"I know. Honestly, I think the most difficult thing is telling him I'm delaying college for a year. You know how he expects me to graduate on time."

Lia faced her. "Belle, listen to me. I made some mistakes when I was about your age because I listened to my father instead of myself. Grant is a reasonable man. He will understand the college delay. Do the best thing for you and your child. Understand?"

She nodded. "Yes. I will."

"Good." Smiling, she gave Belle a quick hug, then continued. "Zach's making fancy pancakes in the Sandcastle. On the house. I think his ploy is to distract everyone from the storm. You should get breakfast."

"Waffles, too?" Belle adored Zach's fancy pancakes—but not as much as his wacky waffles. And, she *was* hungry. Of course, these days, she was always hungry.

"Your favorite kind."

"Yummy." She stood and headed toward her mom. "I do sort of love that guy," she said. "And that he likes to cook."

Lia grinned. "Me too."

<hr>

AT THE SANDCASTLE, BELLE GLANCED ABOUT AND NOTICED the girls from last night all sitting together—Carol, Ella, and Hannah. As she crossed the restaurant to join them, she saw Maggie and Alice sitting in the corner, chatting and sipping coffee. Maggie's younger kids, Jason and Chloe, were parked at a table nearby. Zach had already supplied them with stacks of fancy pancakes, and they were digging in. Other guests were scattered about the restaurant.

She ducked behind the counter, filled a mug with decaf, and then approached the booth where the girls were. "Hey. May I join you?"

"Sure!" Ella scooted closer to the window.

Belle sat, glancing at their cups. "Need refills?" She started to get up.

"Oh, one cup is plenty for me," Ella told her. "I'm good."

"I don't drink coffee," Carol said.

Belle noticed her soft drink.

Hannah shook her head. "I'm a tea girl, and I'm good right now."

"Okay." Belle eased back into her seat. "Well, then."

Suddenly, Zach approached the booth. "Make room for fancy pancakes!" He held a plate in each hand and balanced a third one on his forearm. Setting the first plate in front of Hannah, he said, "I'm dubbing this the Hannah Banana Health Nut Special, since it was your concoction. Banana nut pancakes with organic maple syrup, a dollop of Greek vanilla yogurt on the top, cinnamon sprinkles, with fresh fruit on the side for you, my dear."

Hannah gave him a half-smile. "Goodness. That looks decadent."

Ella piped up. "If you think that's decadent, just wait."

Zach interrupted. "And for you, Miss Ella, the Sinful Banana Ella. Banana split fancy cakes with strawberry glaze, pineapple marmalade, powdered sugar, milk chocolate drizzle, crusty sugared pecans, and whipped cream... Topped off with a brandy-soaked maraschino cherry, of course." He leaned closer to Ella and whispered. "Don't tell your mom about the brandy."

"Deal." Ella sighed. "Yummy."

Hannah's eyes grew wide. "I'm gaining weight just looking at that."

"And for Miss Carol," Zach said, placing the last plate in front of her. "Candy Cane Carol Fancy Pancakes layered with cream cheese frosting, chopped Snickers bar chunks, and peppermint drizzle topped with a scoop of vanilla bean ice cream, candy cane dust, and thick hot fudge."

Carol smiled wide and clapped her hands as the plate landed in front of her. "Oh my God, Zach. Thank you."

The other girls heaved a sigh.

Hannah exclaimed, "That's a shit ton of calories, girl!"

Carol beamed. "I never gain weight."

"Well, you're lucky."

Zach turned to Belle. "The usual, honey?"

She grinned. "Of course. Wacky Waffles. Syrup on the side? But add a couple of scrambled eggs and two links of sausage. Maybe three eggs.

Protein, you know." Zach never made Wacky Waffles the same way twice, so she was curious what she'd get.

"Of course." He winked. "Give me fifteen minutes or so. The orders are coming in fast and furious."

"I can imagine. You need help in the kitchen?"

He shook his head. "No, Melissa is here, and your mom is helping. I'm good. You stay and have fun with the girls. Your food will be up soon."

He left, and Belle glanced around the table.

Hannah eyed her. "Wow. Are you going to actually eat all that? Why the extra protein?"

Well shit. I might as well tell them. It's not like they probably don't suspect, anyway. Plus, she knew her mother had told their mothers... Belle cleared her throat. "Yes. Eating for two, as they say."

"Excuse me?"

"I'm pregnant."

Carol's fork hit the table a little harder than Belle thought she intended. Looking at her, she saw the teenager's eyes grow wide.

"Seriously?" Carol said. "Does your mom know?"

Ella interjected. "Well, of course her mom knows, Carol. Belle is a grown woman, not a teenager, and she and her mother are close. Why wouldn't she know?" Ella turned to Belle and whispered covertly. "She knows. Right? I thought you'd just gained weight."

"Well, I have gained weight. And yes, Carol, my mom knows."

She glanced at Hannah, who was the only one at the table who seemed disinterested in her news. Eyes downcast, she kept on eating her banana nut fancy cakes.

"Do you want to talk about it?" Ella asked.

"Maybe later."

"Well," Carol said, "I, for one, want details."

Ella laughed. "You sounded just like your mother right then, Carol."

"Uh. No."

"Well, you did."

With a frown, Carol dug into her Candy Cane Cakes. "I did not," she said under her breath, chewing rapidly.

Belle glanced at Ella, who rolled her eyes at Carol.

"So, yes. I'm like in my eighth month."

Hannah scooped a forkful of banana pancake into her mouth. "Seriously? You're not showing that much for eight months. I never would have known."

Belle shrugged. "These romper suits are not only comfortable but concealing. Plus, I swim most days, so I haven't gained much weight beyond the baby weight."

"And the romper is super cute," Carol added.

Ella leaned in, ignoring her, it seemed. "So, tell us about the father. I didn't know you were seeing anyone. Is he local?"

Quickly, Belle shook her head. "No, he's not."

"Well, spill it, Belle," Carol said. "We want the juicy details."

Ella huffed and darted a look toward the younger girl. "I'm going to start calling you Maggie Jr."

"Don't you dare!"

Belle jumped in before Carol exploded. "There isn't much to tell—no juicy tidbits, to be honest. He was a guest at the inn. It was right as the season started. Come Monday morning, he was gone, and I've not heard from him since. End of story."

"A one-night hookup. Wow. I didn't know you had it in you."

Belle glared at Carol. *The little witch.* "Well, obviously, I did."

Hannah looked up then. "But you have records here, right? Can't you find him? He deserves to know."

Belle nodded. "Turns out he was a brother of guests, so I don't have details."

"But..." Hannah insisted, "you have *their* information."

"True. I did try calling the number they gave."

"And...?" Hannah prodded.

"And they told me he wasn't there, they didn't know where he was, and not to call back."

Once more, Hannah nudged. "Try another way. I can't believe you gave up so easily."

Belle took offense to that. She had tried another time, and the Cooper's number came up disconnected. Leaning closer to the table, she said softly, but directly. "It's not that I gave up, I just haven't pursued it again. There is plenty of time for me to get in touch with him, if I can. What's he going to do right now, anyway? Nothing." Pausing, she glared at Hannah. "Besides, I don't want to talk to him."

"I get that," Hannah said, "But he has a right to know and make that decision. Perhaps he needs to mull it over and think about his options."

"*His* options?"

"What he wants to do about it and all."

Belle's stomach twisted. Right now, she wasn't sure she could eat a wacky waffle or anything. "He has nothing to do with it. I'm having the baby. Later, he can decide if he wants to take part in his child's life, or not."

"He has rights." Hannah stared.

"And I have the right to pick the time to share this news with him." Belle frowned back at Hannah and suddenly wondered why she was even arguing with her. "It's my situation, my decision. And if I decide not to look for him, that's my decision too. Honestly, it would make things much easier for me."

"But—"

Belle leaned further over the table. "But it's my story to tell, if and when I decide to do that. He obviously isn't interested in me, or he would have made some contact by now."

A memory flashed through Belle's head at those words. Their last kiss, his promise to call her the next night... Then radio silence.

Hannah started to say something, then sighed and went back to her pancakes. "Fine," she muttered. "It's your life."

"Exactly."

Carol leaned in. "But you have his name, right? Google him."

"That makes me feel like a stalker."

"Then we'll do it." Ella gave Belle a hard look. "What's his name? We can help."

"Absolutely." Hannah pushed her plate away. "Like I said, he deserves to know. Besides, I like to solve a good mystery and what else are we going to do this weekend? Wait for Santa and play reindeer games?"

Belle rolled her eyes. The last thing she wanted was to tell them his name. "I don't know. We do have Monopoly." That was an attempt to lighten up the discussion, but she wasn't sure it hit the mark. All this talk was making her nervous. "Look, I need to be ready and I'm not sure I am. I'm not dropping that bombshell on him at Christmas."

"Not saying you have to do it this weekend," Hannah urged. "But you need to consider when and how you want to share the news with him. And I think…" she glanced about the table, her gaze lingering on Ella and Carol, "that we can all help you with this. Just talk it through. Have you really discussed with anyone besides your mother?"

Belle hadn't. And while her mother and Jenn were both supportive, did she need some other friends to lean on and talk with occasionally, too? Glancing about the table, she had to wonder—were these girls the friends she'd recently longed for?

Surely not. Right?

Belle glanced off to see her mother scurrying across the restaurant. By the time she got to their table, she was nearly out of breath. "Belle. We need to look at room availability again. Do we have any suites?"

"I checked earlier, remember?" She noticed her mother's frown. Something was up. "We have one, I believe."

"Good. We need to move Sam, Julia, and Hannah into that one."

Hannah perked up. "What?"

Lia faced her. "I've already talked with your dad. We're moving you out of the Gull Cottage to higher ground because of the storm."

"Oh!" Hannah shifted in her seat. "I should go help them."

"Eat your breakfast. I think they are about to finish up. Zach sent housekeeping staff. You're in suite 304 now. I'll get you a key in a few minutes." She slid her gaze to Belle again. "But we need more rooms. How many left?"

"I think one cottage, the Sandpiper, and a room on the second floor. Maybe two."

"The Sandpiper is closest to the hotel, so it might be safe from the storm surge. We'll put the fishermen in there."

"Fishermen?"

A breath whooshed from Lia's mouth. "Apparently some of Zach's friends from New Hampshire came down for a fishing expedition, now canceled. They were expecting to spend a few days out at sea. Well, not now, and they need a place to stay."

"How many?"

"Three men, and apparently one has a son with him."

"We could clean up a suite real fast. One they haven't started painting yet. That is, if you think a cottage is iffy because of flooding."

"Let me talk to Zach." Lia started to hustle off, then turned back. "Oh, and I almost forgot...."

As her mother faced her, Belle noticed the wrinkles across her forehead and her pursed lips. A thud landed in the pit of her stomach. The look on her mother's face was rather odd. "Mom?"

"Your dad just called."

"Dad?"

"Yes."

"And?"

"He's on his way here."

"What? Here?" She pushed herself up and out of the booth.

Lia nodded. "They landed in Norfolk about thirty minutes ago."

"They?" *Crap.* Not only her dad, but his entire new family? Glancing down at herself, she cradled her baby bump under the romper. Would he be able to tell that she was pregnant? Would he be upset that she'd not told him? *Dammit.* She was not ready to talk to her dad yet—let alone with an audience.

"He said Ginger and one of her kids came, too. Think the last rooms will be okay for them?"

"Of course. Which kid?"

"Luna."

Belle exhaled slowly, temporarily relieving the ache in her gut. Luna was her age, but they were so very different—she was much more of a free spirit than Belle would ever be—and they'd not had many opportunities to get to know each other. "Shit."

"Now, Belle."

"I'm not sure I'm in the mood for Ginger and Luna right now." She glanced down and placed a hand on her abdomen. "Or Dad."

"You still haven't told him."

"No."

"Well, get ready."

"I... I don't think I'm in the right place to do that. Can we find them another hotel or something?"

"Belle!" Lia squared herself. "In this storm? No. Besides, he's your father. We don't do that. You think I'm in the mood to spend Christmas with my ex-husband and his new wife and her family?"

"No." Belle muttered. Suddenly, she realized how awkward this was going to be for her mom, too. And probably Zach. *Christmas chaos indeed*. "Fine. The more the merrier, I guess. I will tell him as soon as I see him."

"As if he will not realize it by looking at you."

"Right."

"Right." Lia met Belle's gaze and held it for several heartbeats, then trotted off.

Slowly, Belle faced the girls at the table.

Hannah rose, her gaze locked with Belle's—she could almost feel the judgement in her demeanor. "Another man in your life you've left clueless, Belle?"

Belle met her stare head on. "Oh, shut up. Eat your damn Hannah Banana pancakes."

Eight

An hour later, Lia stood in the second-floor office—Zach on one side of her, Belle on the other—staring at Grant, his wife Ginger, and his step-daughter, Luna. Awkward introductions were exchanged—and since this was the first time this family configuration had come together—Lia had to admit she was anxious.

And perhaps a little worried.

Maybe uneasy was a better word.

It wasn't that she and Grant had a difficult relationship, or that she was jealous of Ginger—it was none of that. Her uneasiness was simply related to the awkwardness of the growing situation, their pregnant daughter, people showing up unexpectedly, and no room at the inn.

And on Christmas Eve, no less.

"Since you decided not to come to Seattle," Grant said, looking at Belle, "We thought we would come to you. Ginger's younger kids are with their father this weekend, so it was easier for us to get away—and you've talked about how lovely Tuckaway Bay is, so we were eager to see it."

At that moment, a gust of wind hit the windows of the hotel office, rattling them, and shaking the entire structure on its pilings.

The entire group froze for a split second.

Lia jerked and grasped Zach's arm.

"Of course, we had no clue about this storm when we booked our flight and hotel," Grant continued.

Zach cleared his throat. "Well, let's get you all settled. Grant, I might need your help if you're up to it. I know it's a long flight from Seattle and you could be jet lagged, so just say the word if you're not. I have some other guys coming soon, too. I'd like to get the ocean side windows boarded up here at the restaurant, and also on the hotel, if we can. We're probably starting late."

"And sandbags around the Gull Cottage," Lia added.

"Right."

Grant stepped forward and put out his hand. "It's the least I can do since we are at your mercy. Besides, after a four-hour flight, I would love to move around some. We booked a room down the road at the Carolina Blue Motel, so we wouldn't impose here, but...."

"But the Carolina is closed up tight, I imagine," Zach said. "They are closer to the ocean than we are and often suffer storm damage. They've likely evacuated."

"Yes. Ginger had a voice mail on her phone when we landed. We could see the place was empty when we drove by, so we came here instead."

Lia stared at Grant, glanced at Zach, then back again to her ex-husband. "Well, that was ridiculous anyway. We have a room here. It's not huge, but it's clean. Two double beds with a microwave and a small refrigerator. It's not ocean front so you're protected from the storm...somewhat."

At this rate, listening to the roaring winds, she wasn't sure anywhere on the beach was totally protected.

Grant held her gaze, then looked at his wife. "We're not picky."

"It will be perfect." Ginger stepped forward. "We appreciate it and know this is an imposition. Our flight was the last one they let land before they shut down the airport in Norfolk. We could barely get a rental car. I can't tell you how grateful we are."

Lia stepped forward and grasped Ginger's hand. "No worries. You all will be safe and dry here. If you haven't had breakfast yet, head over to the restaurant."

"Good idea," Zach said. "We should all eat a hot meal before we lose power."

Lia twisted to stare at her husband. "Zach?"

He shrugged. "It might happen. We need to be ready."

Her heart pounded a little. "Do we have a generator?"

"Yes. And some battery-powered lamps and such. We need to make sure everything is charged up before the full force of this storm hits. And that includes phones."

Grant stepped forward. "When do you expect that to happen? We're happy to help."

"Absolutely," Ginger added.

"Thanks." Zach jerked a nod. "Let's get you settled in your room first and then meet downstairs at the Sandcastle for breakfast. We'll plan from there."

"Gotta love a man with a plan," Grant said.

Lia closed her eyes momentarily. Was this really happening? Her ex-husband and her current husband working together? How did this happen?

"I'll get your room keys," Belle said. "And point you in the right direction."

Lia looked at Belle, who focused on her father. "Good idea, honey."

"And then I'll meet you back here to walk you to the Sandcastle," Belle added. Turning to Zach, she added, "You still have my waffles?"

"Coming up. Five minutes."

"Good. I'm hungry."

Zach trotted off without a word. Lia wondered if all of this would be too much for him—or would he just weather the storm, so to speak, in typical Zach fashion? He was used to this, right? The chaos from stormy weather in the Outer Banks? Surely, he and Aunt Grace had hunkered down many times over the years.

But not the chaos that family dynamics can bring into play with the holidays.

Girlfriends. Kids. A pregnant stepdaughter. His new wife's unexpected ex-spouse, and his new family....

Maybe it wasn't Zach. Maybe this was all just too much for her.

Turned out, she had little time to dwell on it.

With Belle getting Grant and his new family settled into their room, Lia returned to the restaurant to see if she could help Zach with breakfast. Her gut told her they should get that done quickly so they could concentrate on battening down the hatches.

And no sooner had she had that thought, had the double doors to the restaurant pushed open with a bang, and four men stumbled inside, wind and rain nipping at their backsides.

They dropped their gear inside the door, water dripping from their slickers and puddling around their boots. One of the men shouted out loudly. "Whooo is in da house! Who in da house *now*!"

Zach turned, having just delivered Belle's waffles, and shouted louder than she'd ever heard him bellow before. "*We* be in da house!"

And the other men chimed along too. "We be in da house! We be in da house *now*!"

Zach raced across the room and bear-hugged the first man. The others patted backs. All of them were shouting simultaneously. Lia slowly approached the group and stood slightly behind Zach.

"Monk, you asshole!" Zach blurted out.

"What's that around your middle, T-Man? An apron?" The man Zach had called Monk tugged at his apron string. Zach batted his hands away and danced a few steps backward.

T-Man? Lia had never heard anyone call him that before.

Another man pushed a forefinger into Zach's middle. "What's this, dough boy? A little pudge around the middle? Married life is good, I see." He winked at Lia.

She gave a half grin back.

"It's all good, man," Zach turned to him. "Otter, you S.O.B. Been too long." Zach gave him a hug too.

Zach glanced at the third man. "You too, Chuckers." He paused and stared at the younger man standing beside him. "Wait. This isn't Josh, is it?"

Lia took in his wide grin of recognition. "Yep. It's me, Uncle T."

"Damn." Zach shook his head. "Been too long. I thought you were still like, twelve, or something."

"Naw. I'm twenty-two, Uncle T." Josh rubbed his chin and grinned.

Zach shook his head. "Too damn long."

"For all of us," Monk said.

"That's why we planned the trip. Wanted to bring the boy, too." Chuckers put his arm around his son, Josh.

"Except we didn't think we'd be stranded here island side. We were out for wrestling a few bluefins, you know?"

"Helluva good time for tuna, I'm told."

"Yeah, well, not today, T-Man."

"And I'm sorry about that, man. The weather... You just never know."

The men kept chatting, patting backs, and exchanging bear hugs.

Lia suddenly became aware of someone standing beside her. After a moment, Belle leaned in and whispered. "The fishermen, I presume?"

Nodding slowly, Lia said, "Yes. Otherwise known as his college hockey team. Or some of them anyway."

Belle exhaled so loudly Lia could feel the breath on her arm. "We have our work cut out for us."

"Apparently so."

"The one guy doesn't look old enough to have played hockey with Zach in college."

Lia shook her head. "You're right. I think he's the son of the one called Chuckers."

"Chuckers?"

"Um, hmm. So far I've detected a Monk, an Otter, a Chuckers, and then Josh, the young guy. Zach, evidently, is called T-Man."

"Interesting."

"Yes."

"I can't wait to hear that story...." Lia glanced over at Belle—but something, or someone, had caught her daughter's eye.

WHEN HER FATHER, GINGER, AND LUNA CAME DOWNSTAIRS, Belle hadn't quite finished her waffles. They had insisted they could find the Sandcastle on their own and wandered down about twenty minutes after Belle had shown them the way.

Even though it was really good to see him, she'd managed to avoid conversation with her dad to any degree—regarding anything other than finding their room, and so on—but as they approached where she sat at a booth near the kitchen door, she knew that the conversation was imminent.

"Come here and give me a hug, you." Her dad bellowed out as he approached.

Belle pushed out of the booth and quickly went to her dad, throwing her arms around his neck. He squeezed her so tight she almost jerked back, worried about the baby. Obviously, he could feel her baby bump, right? But he said nothing. Ginger and Luna stood a few steps behind. Belle smiled over her dad's shoulder.

"I've missed you, Dad," she whispered.

"Oh, sweet girl, I've missed you more." His breath was warm and tickly on the side of her cheek.

She pulled back. "Hungry?"

"Starving."

"Us, too." Ginger stepped forward and also gave Belle a hug. "It's good to see you."

"You, too." Tossing a glance at Luna, she added, "How are you?"

"Literally dying of boredom here, but fine. I'm okay," Luna blurted out. "No worries."

Well, okay then....

Belle motioned toward the booth. "Let's sit. I'm finishing up my pancakes."

Luna scooted into the side of the booth where she had been sitting earlier, then Belle tucked herself in beside her. Grant and Ginger sat opposite them.

"We have menus," Belle explained, "But mostly we just tell the server what we want. Zach's been making fancy pancakes this morning for the guests, which pretty much means anything goes."

"Interesting," Ginger said. "Such as?"

"Well, I had wacky waffles. They were waffles with bananas, peppermint syrup, and chocolate chips, plus a couple of scrambled eggs and sausages on the side."

"Good gracious!" Ginger took a quick glance at Luna. "We're vegan, you know. Luna and I. Think he can accommodate?"

"I'm sure he can. Just tell him what you want. If it's in the pantry, he can cook it."

Grant cleared his throat and leaned toward Belle. "That's a lot of food. Are you still swimming?"

Shit. Here it comes. "I am, but not as much."

"Your leg?"

"Oh no. Just reworking my routine."

"I see." Her dad's gaze landed hard and steady on hers. He paused, as though he was waiting for her to elaborate. In fact, he paused so long Belle feared the silence between them would shatter into a million pieces.

"So, Dad. There's this thing I need to tell you."

"Umhmm."

Belle nodded slowly. "Yes. I'm... You see, last spring...."

Luna slapped the table, commanding all their attention. "Good God, Belle. Quit being such a baby and tell him. You're not a child. He already knows anyway."

"Luna!" Ginger grabbed her daughter's hand. "That was uncalled for."

Belle stared at her father, who met her gaze with an equal level of intensity.

"Well?" he prompted.

"Okay. I'm pregnant."

"I know."

"How? Mom?"

He shook his head. "No."

Belle felt perplexed. "I wanted you to hear this from me, which is why I haven't talked about it yet. I wanted to do it in person. But I've been really private about my...situation, so I don't understand how...."

"Ned Speakman."

Panic gripped Belle's heart. "When? Why? Is something wrong?"

"No. No, honey." He grasped her hand on the table. "I saw him at the old club in Chicago, at a benefit golf tournament back in July. He thought I knew."

Oh hell. "And you've known all this time and said nothing?"

He sat back and heaved out a long sigh. "Just waiting for you, sweetheart. Now, tell me you are okay, and fill me in on the details."

Carol & Maggie

Nine

CHRISTMAS EVE
Between 9 a.m. and Midnight

"PERSONALLY, I CAN'T BELIEVE SHE TOLD YOU TO SHUT UP."

Carol Oliver watched the developing scene on the other side of the restaurant with interest—in particular, eyeing the group of fishermen who had arrived a few minutes earlier. The young guy in the group was effing hot—and if she had to be stuck here for the weekend, well, a hot guy was a plus.

Her gaze drifted to Belle and her father, Grant Mitchell, whom Carol had not seen in years. She remembered him from before, when Lia and Grant were still married. That was probably a dozen years or more ago, and she'd been...what? Maybe five? Belle motioned for her father, a woman, and a girl about her age to join her at a booth near the kitchen.

Hmm. I should investigate—does Grant have a new girlfriend? The trio, plus Belle, sat and chatted, although Carol couldn't hear what they were saying.

Damn it.

She turned to Hannah. "Right? That was so freaking rude of her."

"She's hormonal," Hannah said with a shrug. "No big deal. Besides, I sort of provoked it."

"Well, she was bitchy, to be sure. God, I never want to get pregnant."

Ella laughed. "To be honest, I don't want to be around if you ever get pregnant. You're moody enough on a normal day."

"I am not!" She sat straight up.

"Yeah, you sort of are," Ella shot back.

"All right, girls. Cool it." Hannah glanced toward the window. "Looks like we're stuck inside all day."

Carol followed her gaze. The ocean was kicking up huge white caps and rolling higher onto the beach. The sky was an odd shade of purple and navy blue, with green tinges near the horizon. Wind and sand hit the windows with force. "I think you are right. I may have to hit up on the cute guy over there. Did you see him?"

Ella and Hannah looked at the guy again.

"I suppose he's nice looking," Ella said.

Hannah shrugged her shoulders. "He's a guy."

Carol sighed. "You two are impossible. He's freaking hot."

"And older than you, Carol," Ella shared. "You are jailbait to him."

"I'm seventeen! And we'll see about that." *Quit being so damn smug, Ella.*

"Okay, ladies. Look. We're stuck here, so let's make the best of it. We're not chasing boy toys, and we're going to get along. Right? No drama."

Carol turned back and narrowed her gaze, first glancing at Ella—sweet, smart, always the good girl, Ella—and then Hannah, whom she hadn't quite nailed yet, personality-wise. She was sort of bossy, though. "Girl, drama is my middle name."

"See?" Ella said. "You *are* just like your mother. I swear, she keeps my mother spun up into a tizzy most of the time."

"Well, maybe your mother needs to keep her nose out of my mother's business."

"And perhaps *your* mother," Ella shot back, "should figure out her life so *my* mother doesn't have to worry. I mean, she and Lia and Julia are always anxious about everything going on between her and your dad. And whether or not you realize it, you are just like her—helpless, vulnerable, gullible, and self-centered."

For a moment, Carol was kind of shocked, speechless even. *How fucking dare she? What do they know about my mom and dad?* Then Ella's last words hit her, and the heat of anger flushed up her neck to her cheeks. She pushed at Hannah. "Let me out."

Hannah braced herself against the table. "Wait."

"Why? I don't need to stay here and be insulted."

Ella leaned forward. "Sit back, Carol. What are you going to do, anyway? There's nothing going on. The Sandcastle is the only place where anything is happening. In fact, I may just sit here until lunch, and then dinner."

"Well, that's an exciting life." Carol rolled her eyes, shifting her gaze toward the guy again.

"That's me. Boring Ella."

"Just like your mom," Carol bit back. "Boring, mother hen, Alice."

Ella shot Carol a look. "Why do you say that?"

"Because that's what my mom always says. In fact, she makes fun of your mom behind her back because she's such a goody-two-shoes."

Hannah laughed. "I haven't heard that phrase since I was a kid."

Ella stood up. "And your mother screws any guy in a pickup truck who is the opposite of your dad!"

"Whoa." Hannah shot daggers at Ella. "That's a lot uncalled for."

"She does not!" Carol batted at Hannah. "Let me out now."

Hannah pushed out of the booth.

Carol passed.

Ella stomped off toward the restroom.

Hannah followed.

Oh, no you don't. Within seconds, Carol caught up with Ella in the hallway, grabbed her arm, swung her around, and stood nose-to-nose with her. "And your mother is a...a...."

Ella stood her ground. "A what? Cat got your tongue? Hard to find anything to pin on my mom since she's such a goody-two-shoes?"

Carol wanted to blast her. Ella was always so...good. She was an honor student, or so her mother said. And she was pretty and popular. Her mother reminded her of that often. *Why can't you be more like Ella?* She would say. Ella never got into trouble at school, and she was going to college on an academic scholarship.

"*Your* mother...."

"Yes?"

Carol took another step and peered into Ella's perfect blue eyes. "Your mother humps women. She's a lesbian, and she's been hiding it from you for years. So how about that? Think she's perfect now?"

Hannah quickly interrupted. "Whoa. There's nothing wrong with being a lesbian."

Ella paused, studying Hannah. "Of course not."

"You an expert on that?" Carol arched her left brow.

"I have some knowledge. Yes. What of it?"

"So you like humping girls, too?"

"God!" Ella shouted. "Carol, stop. Of course, she's not. You're being a bitch."

"No, it's okay, Ella," Hannah said, looking directly at Carol. Reaching out, she touched Carol's arm. "While it is absolutely none of your business, you are right. I am gay."

Carol pushed Hannah's hand away. "Well, congratulations to you."

"That's so immature, Carol. Good God." Ella turned to Hannah. "I'm sorry."

"Ella, Carol is just misinformed, I believe," Hannah said.

"I mean, I'm sorry I said of course you weren't gay and...oh, crap. I'm so confused."

"It's probably because your mother kept the truth from you," Carol told her. "Right Hannah?"

Hannah shook her head and glanced off.

"Hiding it from you wasn't very cool," Carol bit out.

Hannah stepped between the girls. "Time to pause, ladies. Carol, take a breath."

"You don't tell me what to do." *Who did she think she is, anyway?*

Ella stepped away. "I would know if my mother was gay."

"Ask her. See if she tells you."

"How do you know this, Carol?"

Because I'm good at finding out shit. "I hear things."

Hannah grasped Ella's hand, an attempt to divert her attention, Carol thought. *Well, good luck.*

"Look," she said. "Your mother is from another generation. It's possible she's not ready to come out yet, and when to tell you might be something she's trying to figure out—if this is true, that is. Let her."

"Good grief. What's the fuss?" Carol rolled her eyes.

"Because coming out is a big deal." Hannah glared. "I didn't know you were such an expert on LGBTQ+ issues."

"I'm not and I don't pretend to be. So, she likes girls. Women. No big deal."

"God, Carol! Shut up."

"But hiding it is dishonest."

"Like I said, she's not ready."

"Stop!" Ella shouted. "Just shut up about it. Okay! Stop talking."

Inwardly, Carol wanted to laugh and giggle like a hyena. She liked seeing Ella squirm. But on the outside, she didn't want to show her giddy emotion. "Fine. Look. Have a great day, ladies. I'm off for an adventure."

"You better not go outside, Carol. The storm."

She twisted back, speaking over her shoulder. "Oh, what I have planned will definitely take place somewhere hot and steamy."

"Condoms, Maggie, use them," Ella barked.

"Quit mother henning me, Alice."

AFTER BREAKFAST WITH ALICE, MAGGIE MADE HER WAY back to her suite to check in with Max. She glanced at her phone—they had ten minutes until their family face-to-face call.

Jason and Chloe were playing in their room of the two-bedroom suite, laughing and rough housing a bit too much, but with all the sugar they'd had for breakfast, why should she expect anything different? She'd ask Zach not to make fancy pancakes for them tomorrow.

But wait. No.

She thought back to earlier, when her kids were digging into the sugary, syrupy, gooey, messes of pancakes and toppings, and enjoying every bite. Max never let them have sugar. She'd thought then about how angry he would have been, if he were there.

They are growing children, Maggie. They don't need sugar.

Once in a while doesn't hurt, Max.

Oh sure. And are you going to deal with the aftermath of fidgeting, running, yelling kids? Or am I?

Of course, he never would have agreed to fancy pancakes in the first place, if he were here—and she'd learned that his *dealing with the aftermath* was never pleasant. So, she always waited until he was out of town to let them have sweets.

But if by some fluke he had let them, and the kids were rough-housing like they were at the moment, he would have turned angry—and taken it out on her eventually because she'd allowed the pancakes to happen.

Most things were her fault.

With a sigh, she breathed deep and sat on the edge of the bed.

She didn't have to worry about that right now, though, did she? Because Max was far away, and he would not be home for weeks.

With another long exhale, Maggie closed her eyes and let the relief wash over her. She sat there for a moment, listening to her children's laughter in the other room, knowing she should go in there and quiet them down, but smiled gently instead. They were having fun. Good.

Get through the call, Maggie, and remember he can't reach through the computer. He's half a world away.

They'd scheduled the call for ten o'clock that morning, Christmas Eve, eastern U.S. time, which was midnight in Brisbane. Jason thought it was cool when Max mentioned that he'd have Christmas fourteen hours before the rest of them. They'd arranged for a Zoom call then, at midnight his time, so they could all say Merry Christmas together.

She'd promised the kids they could open one gift during the call—the one from Max. They didn't know she'd bought it, and that Max didn't even know what was in the box.

Had Max ever bought a present? She didn't think so.

Maggie knew Jason was looking forward to the call. At thirteen, he was doing more with his dad, like playing golf. It worried her that her sweet boy was spending too much time with his self-important, and often-misogynistic father. She didn't want Jason to grow up disrespecting women or take on Max's attitudes about women in general.

But what kind of example had she set within the family, letting Max rule over and belittle her in front of the kids? A terrible one.

She had to do better—not only for Jason, but also for the girls.

She hoped Chloe didn't get upset during the call. The youngest of her children, the six-year-old had developed no sort of bond or relationship with Max—not that Max had made any attempt. He'd been angry when Maggie found out she was pregnant for the third time. Birth control was her responsibility, and he'd pushed for an abortion.

She'd refused—and had taken the brunt of his anger frequently because of it.

Consequently, he pretty much ignored Chloe and as a result, Maggie wondered if her girl sensed it and felt non-existent around him.

Of course, Carol was the one who commanded the lion's share of his attention. Ever since the incident at Tequila Sunrise a couple of summers ago—she'd played up the "daddy's little girl" bit to the hilt.

It would be no different during this call.

Hopefully today, the self-absorbed teenager would be civil to everyone.

After all, it was Christmas. There were gifts to be had. She'd be there with bells on. Carol liked nothing better than being showered with gifts and attention.

Maggie glanced at her phone again. Speaking of....

Last time she saw her daughter was in the restaurant, eating breakfast with Belle, Ella, and Hannah. She hoped those young ladies would be a positive influence on her this weekend.

She sent a quick text, reminding Carol of the call, then set the phone aside and opened her tablet. It took a minute to find the link and open the software. All she had to do now was gather the children and wait for Max.

She peeked in the bedroom at Chloe and Jason. They were playing a game of "hot lava" and jumping from bed to bed—something she would never have allowed at home. Quietly, she closed the door and left them alone, smiling at their laughter.

Her heart was full.

Drifting toward the window, Maggie watched the ocean roll and crash into the shore. The weather was menacing, and she hoped Zach was monitoring the situation. Looking to the right, she saw movement around the Gull Cottage—the one closest to the ocean. It looked like Sam and Julia and a few of the staff were moving luggage into the hotel. Then, a pickup truck backed close to the cottage porch—as close as the asphalt drive would let him get, she supposed, keeping off the sand— and Zach hopped out with another man and started dragging sandbags toward the porch.

Maggie released a breath. Things didn't look good.

This could be a disastrous Christmas, after all.

Should they head home before the brunt of the storm hit the coast tomorrow? Since they would head inland and west, perhaps they should.

But honestly, she didn't want to. She was here, at the beach, with the people she cared about the most. Why would she want to be anywhere else? Even with this storm?

Maybe it would blow out to sea.

Watching the commotion outside, though, her mind drifted to Christmases past, especially the ones when Carol was little. She was such a joy back then, sweet and funny. Max was good to them both—he was a different man then. Oh, he had his quirks and demands, and he'd made the open marriage arrangement quite clear from the beginning, but he had always treated her well.

Things changed when Jason was born—Max became abruptly moody and distant, and started belittling her in front of others, for no apparent reason. Just because he could. Nothing she did was good enough anymore. Meals. Her clothes. Her weight, hair color, pedicures... Then, after Chloe came into the world, he became angrier and abusive—emotionally, but occasionally physically. Specifically, the past couple of years.

Besides the children, what had changed between them? Was it her?

Or was it him?

Did Max feel like his life was speeding out of control? That the years were slipping away? Was he diving into a mid-life crisis? She couldn't be sure. What were the signs, anyway?

The kids were getting older and had minds of their own, of course. That seemed to aggravate him. Maggie had tired of the homemaker routine and found other things to occupy her days, like joining the Y and taking a painting class. But Max hated change and if she wasn't home in time to get his seven-p.m. dinner on the table, he pouted like a child and the entire family suffered.

She stopped doing things outside the house when he was home. When he was traveling, she'd found other...um...activities.

At least she had several months ago.

That was over now.

With a heavy sigh, she glanced toward the desk and at the tablet. Max still wasn't there.

Carol rushed inside the room. The heavy metal door slammed shut behind her. "Are we on?"

"Not yet."

"Good." She rushed to the desk and looked at the tablet. "Want me to hit the link?"

"Sure." Maggie called out. "Jason! Chloe! Time to call your dad. Come here, please." Maggie gave her daughter a once-over. "Are your clothes wet? Have you been outside?"

Carol laughed and glanced over her shoulder. "No! Spilled my water. Tell you more later."

"Oh." Somehow, Maggie knew there was more to that story.

The two younger ones came bounding into the room, laughing and excited. They crowded up to the desk next to Carol. Maggie noticed the eye roll she made toward her siblings as she removed the three gifts from the desk drawer.

"Everything is ready," Carol said. She glanced up at Maggie. "What time is it?"

"Just a minute past."

The four of them stared at the screen. Max didn't appear.

Maggie lifted her phone off the desk and stepping away from the kids, texted Max.

Maggie: *Max. It's time for the call.*

No response. She waited one minute. The kids were excitedly chatting. Max still hadn't logged in.

Maggie: *Max? The kids are waiting. Call please?*

Silence.

Maggie: *Max? Please don't disappoint them. It's Christmas Eve, dammit!*

The three dots jumped under the text. Finally, he responded.

Max: *Sorry. Fell asleep. Can't make it.*

You goddamned bastard. Anger and disappointment for the kids stewed up inside her. She didn't even bother responding.

"Kids? Your dad just texted. He's tied up and can't make the call now. He'll try tomorrow."

Carol whirled. "What? At freaking midnight? What the eff?"

"Watch your mouth. The littles." She glared at Carol.

"But why?" Carol quipped. "Makes no sense."

A sudden pang knifed into her chest. She'd been thinking the same damn thing. "I don't know."

"It's okay," Jason said, shrugging. He'll call back. "Chloe, let's go play."

Chloe giggled. "Okay. Don't step in the lava!"

Carol shot her mother a look. "Are you letting them play that?"

"It's fine."

"But wait! Can we at least open these presents?" Carol pleaded. "I mean, he would want us to, right?"

Maggie sighed. "Of course. Grab the one with your name on it and let's go sit on the bed. Jason! Chloe! Come back."

The kids snatched up their gifts, and Maggie set the tablet aside. On one hand, she was furious with Max for ditching them. On the other, she had them all to herself, and was thrilled the kids just didn't seem to care that their dad was absent.

EARLIER, ABOUT THE TIME CAROL WAS READY TO MAKE A move on the hot guy, two things happened. One, Josh made an announcement and two, her mother texted.

Their timing sucked.

She'd watched Hannah lead Ella out of the Sandcastle, gave them a sneer behind their backs, and then sat on a stool at the old-fashioned soda counter. The server asked what she wanted, and Carol ordered a glass of ice water. She needed no more sugar after the candy cane fancy cakes.

She was already feeling twitchy from her sugar high.

Crossing her legs, she twirled around on the stool and looked out into the restaurant. The breakfast crowd was thinning. Her mother and Alice had left a while ago—before she and Ella got into their argument —which was a good thing. For some reason, she wanted to get under Ella's skin, but she wasn't willing to suffer her mother's wrath at the moment, or bring Alice into the mix, either.

She wondered… Had Ella gone off to tell her mother what she'd said yet? She supposed she'd know by the fireworks.

Her lips curled into a smile. Now, that would be a scene she would like to witness.

Her gaze drifted to the table of four men not too far away. The fishermen—supposedly Zach's friends from New Hampshire. The older guys had made a rowdy entrance, but the young guy was pretty quiet. While the men laughed and joked and ate their breakfasts, he sort of kept to himself, nodding once and again, and eating his eggs and gravy biscuits—oblivious to his surroundings.

And her.

Well, let's change that.

Twirling back to face the counter, she swiped her arm to the left and her plastic glass of ice water went tumbling over the edge, water splashing onto the floor, and a few fishermen—with ice cubes skating across the tile floor like hockey pucks.

"Oh! My goodness!"

Carol jumped off the stool and snatched up the glass, but it was slippery and shot out of her hand—accidentally, of course—toward hot guy's chair. In fact, it landed right beneath it. The server behind the counter rushed toward her with a towel.

"I got this, sweetie."

She shot the woman a *back off* smirk, snatched the towel from her hand, and nudged her aside.

With her gaze locked on him, she made a beeline toward hot guy.

"Oh shoot. You are all wet. I am so sorry!"

The second she reached his chair—and he turned and met her gaze...*oh damn, big brown eyes*—she stepped on an ice cube and her foot flew out from under her. Simultaneously, she grabbed the back of his shirt as he twisted toward her.

They both toppled to the floor. He practically pinned her there, laying across her chest. She loved every inch of his weight angled over hers.

"Oh... My." She gazed up into mocha eyes.

He abruptly pushed back and up. "You okay? Here." He reached out a hand.

"I'm so sorry," she blurted out. *Not really.* "I'm such a klutz."

"Not your fault." He pulled her to her feet.

"Oh geez. We're both wet."

"It's okay," he said, glancing behind him at the table of men.

"I'm still sorry. By the way, I'm Carol."

The men at the table snickered.

"I'm—"

Behind them, the outside door burst open, slamming against the exterior wall. Zach and Sam stomped inside, shaking the rain off them.

"Can I get everyone's attention?" Zach shouted.

Hot guy turned away from her.

Zach said some words, but she wasn't paying attention.

No. No. Not now, Zach!

Her phone pinged in her back pocket, but she ignored it. Who the heck?

Zach rattled on.... "Sorry to say, folks, this is an all-hands-on-deck situation. I need help filling sandbags, placing them around the hotel, and boarding up windows. All help is appreciated. If you want to fill sandbags, see Sam. Anyone else who wants to help, come with me." He turned toward the door, then quickly back again. "Oh, and for the duration and for your help, all meals and rooms are on me. Compliments of the resort. Let's get to it."

Immediately, everyone pushed back from their tables and headed toward Zach and Sam. Hot guy spun on his heel and was gone.

Carol's phone pinged again. She fished it out of her pocket and read the message.

Mom: *Carol, time to call your dad.*

Ten

Maggie lay back on her bed and closed her eyes. It was only ten-thirty in the morning and she already had a headache. Sometimes the sheer thought of a confrontation with Max did that to her.

Jason and Chloe laughed from the other room. A thud sounded against the wall and crackles of laughter went up between them. She smiled, knowing they were having fun, and for the moment, were happy. They'd opened their gifts, tossed them aside, and then went back to playing the hot lava game.

"I still can't believe you're letting them play that," Carol said. "So noisy. Dad would have had a fit by now and calmed them down."

"They're having fun. Don't worry about it."

Carol's eye roll said it all.

Maggie let out a slow breath between pursed lips. Carol was right, though. Max wouldn't have let it go on for very long. But Max wasn't there—and she rather enjoyed their laughter.

Sitting up, she studied Carol at the desk across the room, holding the necklace—the gift from Max—in her hands and fiddling with the chain.

"You know I like silver, not gold. Right?" Carol met her gaze.

"What?"

"The necklace. I always wear silver jewelry."

Well fuck that and the hefty price I paid for gold. Swinging her legs over the side of the bed, Maggie sat up straighter. "I suppose your dad didn't realize."

Carol's gaze didn't waver. "You mean *you* didn't realize."

"The gift was from your dad, Carol."

"Dad knows I like silver." Her daughter stood. "But you bought it. You always buy all the gifts. Dad is too busy working and doing important things. Besides, doing stuff like that is your job, isn't it?"

My job? You mean the menial tasks? The daily grind? The unimportant stuff? Good Lord. She had to set a better example for her children. What kinds of messages was she sending them anyway, about her role in their marriage? The family? Hell, in society?

She stood. "I love taking care of you and your siblings, and if that means I buy the gifts, then so be it. Although, it wouldn't hurt your father to do things like that occasionally."

"He's busy making the money."

"Yes. That's the arrangement." *Shit. Shut up, Maggie.*

Carol tossed her a sneery grin, then set the necklace on the desk. "I'm going back down to the Sandcastle. Zach needs help filling sandbags and stuff. He's asked for everyone's help."

"Oh?"

"Yes. And all the rooms and food are on him now."

She should do her part. "I'll help too."

"Uh…" Carol's smile faded. "You shouldn't, Mom. You can't leave the littles."

Eyeing her daughter, she wondered what that was really about and glanced toward the bedroom. "The kids will be okay here."

Leisurely crossing her arms over her chest—with all the drama she could muster, it seemed—Carol snickered. "Really? They will have that room torn to shreds in an hour."

Maggie cocked her head. "You think so? Jason is thirteen and responsible. They will be fine."

"Keep telling yourself that, Mom."

She sounded way too much like Max right then. *The little witch.*

Maggie squared herself, stared at Carol for a few seconds, then called out, "Jason! Come here, please."

Jason rushed into the room, breathing hard and grinning. "Yeah?"

Maggie quickly rotated and focused on him. "There is a bad storm coming. Zach needs people to fill sandbags and board up windows. Carol and I are going down to help. In an hour or so, she'll come back to watch Chloe, and you'll come down to do your part. Okay? That way, we all will contribute."

He nodded. "Okay, sure Mom."

"Oh, and one more thing. I do not want that room torn up, or any broken bones by jumping on the beds, so no more of that for a while. How about a movie and some popcorn?"

"That works," he said. "Hey Chloe!" He stuck his head in the room.

Chloe bounded out and he told her the plan. She raced him to the TV remote control, and they settled on the sofa.

Turning, Maggie faced Carol and met her still smirky gaze. "Let's go." Grasping her daughter by the elbow, she tucked her hand into the crook. "See you in an hour, Jason."

"Sounds good."

Carol muttered something under her breath and sighed.

Maggie smiled to herself.

THE MOMENT THEY ENTERED THE SANDCASTLE, CAROL realized the place was practically empty. No *hot guy*, sadly. "Well, crap."

"So where is everyone?" Maggie asked.

"I don't know. Probably outside."

"There's Lia. She'll know."

Her mom clutched her hand tighter and led her to where Lia stood behind the counter. Goodness, she had a grip on her. What the hell? She wasn't three anymore.

Time to escape.

"Lia!" Carol called out. "Where are all the...people?"

"Oh, thanks so much for helping." Lia rushed forward and hugged

Maggie. "I don't mind telling you, because you're a friend, that I'm frightened of this storm and the potential damage."

"You have insurance, right?" Maggie asked.

"Sure. But I worry about the damage and what if someone gets hurt?"

"I'm sure you are taking all the precautions."

Lia nodded. "According to Alice, the local government does not feel we need to evacuate, just be preventative."

"Then let's not worry. Okay?"

Carol watched her mother and Lia chat, then let her attention drift to the windows facing the ocean. Men outside on the pool patio struggled with big boards.

"Oh, there are the guys."

"Yes. They've started boarding up the lower levels. Not sure they can get to all the floors. We need more help."

"I'll go," Carol said.

Maggie clutched her hand tighter. "Wait. That's a man's job."

Carol huffed. "This is not 1920, Mom."

Lia smiled at Carol. "Let them take care of that, honey. Sam needs help in the parking lot in front of the hotel loading sandbags. We can't touch the dunes, but there is dry sand under the hotel stored there for this reason, apparently."

"That's what we will do." Her mom caught her eye.

"I'm heading that way now," Lia added. "Follow me."

Fine. Just fine. I'll escape once we get outside.

The wind hit them with force as they left the restaurant and rounded the hotel.

"Good gracious," Lia said. "Those dunes are not doing their job of blocking the wind!"

"Let's just hope they block the storm surge." Maggie ducked under the hotel as another blast hit them. This time with rain. "Geez, I hope we make it through this."

"And today is nothing like what tomorrow is supposed to be like."

"A Christmas storm."

"Yes. Ho, ho, ho!"

Carol listened to their banter and gradually hung back as they moved along the concrete path between the pilings toward the crowd at the opposite end. As her mother and Lia approached Sam, and apparently received their assignments, she ducked behind a set of stairs and through a gap in the dunes to see if she could circle back toward the patio where she'd seen the men earlier.

"Oh, freaking fuck!" She called out, when a gust of wind and rain and sand peppered her face. "What the hell!"

The wind forced her to walk closer to the building as she rounded the dunes and approached the pool, struggling with the wooden gate and stumbling toward the ground level of the hotel. She guarded her face from the little flying projectiles and splayed her palms flat on the wood siding as she inched toward the group. Several feet away, she could see some men battling the boards and pounding with hammers. She wondered if they were getting much accomplished.

If they weren't, they could all go inside, and she could cozy up to the object of her attention.

If she could find him.

"Carol!" Zach rushed toward her. "What the hell are you doing out here?"

"I came to help," she shouted. "What can I do?"

The wind whipped around them—her hair plastered against her face. Pulling the damp strands back with her hand, she stared at Zach.

He glared. "That's ridiculous. Get back inside. Or help with the sandbags."

"But I thought I could be more useful out here." Out of the corner of her eye, she spotted the hot guy. He stood a few feet away now, looking at her and Zach. "Maybe I could help him?"

Zach glanced behind him and then met her gaze again. "No. Go help Sam. Now! I don't have time to fool with you and I don't want you to get hurt. Your dad would kill me. Understand?"

"But—"

"Carol!"

Zach's patience was wearing thin. She'd seen that same expression on other adults before. Probably best not to test his tolerance in the middle of this storm. "Fine!"

She turned and made her way to the path between the dunes, under the motel, bypassed the sandbag crowd, and headed for the stairs. When she got to their suite, dripping from head to toe, she shouted for Jason.

"Your turn! I just got drenched. Going to take a shower and change clothes. The sandbaggers are under the hotel toward the end opposite the Sandcastle. Take the stairs."

Jason rose and looked her over. "You weren't gone long."

"I know. I'll go back later." *Right. When everyone is warm and dry inside.* "Mom wants us to help."

"Okay." He grabbed his jacket off a chair. "Later."

Carol heaved out a breath and glanced at Chloe. "Stay there. I'll be quick."

"'Kay. Can we get more popcorn?"

"Soon as I'm finished."

"'Kay."

She had no concern about Chloe moving an inch. Her eyes were glued to the animated movie.

The shower was warm and relaxing, and honestly, exactly what she needed to calm herself down a few notches. Afterward, she pulled on some yoga pants and a T-shirt and padded into the main room.

"Popcorn?"

She glanced at Chloe. "Sure."

For a few seconds, she busied herself at the microwave, then took the bag of freshly popped corn to Chloe. Instead of joining her on the sofa, she sauntered to the desk and opened her mother's tablet. The call link for her dad was still up. Positioning the tablet upright, she clicked it.

What the hell? If he were there, great. If not, she'd try again tomorrow.

The session opened and the picture on the screen was shadowy dark —but not black, like he hadn't logged on yet. Weird.

No. Wait.

What was that noise? Something squeaky.

He *was* logged on. Had he tried to reach out after they'd left? And maybe forgotten he was still live?

The noise again...like, a baby crying. *What?*

Carol adjusted herself in the desk chair, leaning closer to the tablet. "Dad?"

A woman said something. "Max. Wake up. It's your turn with the baby."

As her eyes adjusted to the blackness on the screen, Carol realized she was looking into the shadows of a dimly lit room. Muffled noises came through the speaker. A light blinked on to the left of the screen, and she watched her father get up out of the bed and stumble across the room.

Dad?

What the ever-loving fuck?

He leaned over a baby crib. *A crib?*

"Come here, sweetie pie. Daddy's here."

Carol couldn't stay still any longer. "Dad! *Dad!* What the fuck?"

He swung around and looked straight at her. "Carol? Shit. What are you...? Fuck."

The woman mumbled. "Max, what?"

"Get up, Lily. Get the fuck up and take the baby."

"Who is *that,* Dad? What are you *doing*?"

He practically shoved the baby in the woman's arms. "Carol, sweetheart, let me explain...."

"Oh shit. That's your daughter, Maxie?"

Maxie? Oh, this is too freakin' insane. "Dad. What the hell. Is that your *baby*? Who is *Lily*?"

"Honey, let me explain. And don't tell your mother. Let me talk to her."

Shit. Shit!

She wasn't often shocked—in fact, she was the one who liked to shock others—but at that moment, she was speechless. The words just wouldn't come...she had no clue what to say to the man that, *up until this moment*, she had adored.

Her heart pounding, her chest muscles squeezing her breath, her brain spun, leaving her lightheaded. With a shaking breath, she clicked off the link and closed the tablet.

Joining Chloe on the sofa, she wrapped them both up in a blanket and hid her tears.

Long after the sandbags were filled and placed around the ground level of the hotel, cottages, and restaurant—and after she'd spent an hour with Lia, Alice, and Julia—Maggie slowly headed back to her suite. The day had worn her out, physically and mentally, and both her legs and her heart felt like lead. The physical part she was not used to—the mental part was more of the same of her life lately.

Hell, who was she kidding? Her emotional life was in constant chaos.

Earlier, Jason had moved from sandbag duty to boarding windows after a while, but as the storm grew darker and increasingly ominous, she'd sent him up to check on the girls. A few minutes later, they'd all stopped at Zach's orders, hoping for the best.

"Everyone rest up, take a shower, and get warm," Zach had told them. "Let's gather back at the Sandcastle in an hour or so for food. Not promising a gourmet meal, but we have sandwiches and potato salad, and cookies and other assorted leftovers from breakfast."

"Christmas Eve smorgasbord?" One of the hockey player fishermen —Maggie couldn't remember his name, Chuck or Huck or Possum or something—called out.

Zach nodded. "Yes, something like that, Chuckers. Let's eat and then call it a day. This storm is gaining speed. Maybe later, we'll rustle up a Christmas Eve dinner."

"Whoa ho! Sounds like a winner," the one called Chuckers exclaimed. "Winner, winner, Christmas dinner!"

But Maggie wasn't feeling so festive...or much like Christmas Eve chumminess with Zach's fishing buddies, and guests she didn't know— she was damned tired and dirty. She turned to Lia. "Okay if I fix some stuff for the kids and me and take it up to the room. I'm dead on my feet right now."

"Of course, Maggie. Do what's best for you."

"I'll fix some sandwiches, grab a few bottles of water, and we will be fine. I'm pooped and hungry, and I know the kids are too."

"Jason did a lot of work today. Zach said he was a big help."

"Oh, that's good."

"Is Carol still with Chloe?"

Maggie exhaled. "Lord, I hope so. If she left Chloe alone, after the day I've had, I'm not sure how I would react."

"Surely, she wouldn't leave Chloe!"

"Lately, I know nothing for certain with that girl. Jason never went back up to relieve her, so I'm hoping she stayed put. But I do need to go check on them."

She was more than eager now to get back to the suite. "I'll get those sandwiches now. I'm sure Jason is starved."

Lia smiled. "He's becoming quite the young man, isn't he?"

Her heart swelled a little. "He's a good kid. Despite his dad."

Maggie caught the sympathetic look on Lia's face, then glanced off.

"Let me pull a package of cookies and other snacks together for you," Lia said after a few seconds.

"Oh, you don't have to. We brought some things."

"Nonsense," Lia said. "Get your sandwiches and I'll gather the other stuff."

"I don't want to be any trouble."

Lia stared at her, then smiled. "You aren't, Maggie! Let me do this. Gracious, you worked your ass off this afternoon!"

"Well, I want us to do our share."

"No worries there. And Zach and I thank you."

Within a few minutes, she'd headed up the elevator to the third floor with a box of sandwiches and snacks. As she pushed inside, she saw Chloe and Carol huddled together on the sofa, sleeping. The shower was running in the kids' bathroom, so she assumed Jason was showering. Outside, the storm kicked up its anger and blew against the sliding glass door to their small deck.

The guys hadn't reached the third-floor windows. Maybe in the morning, Zach had said. Depending.

She set the box of food down on the table.

For a moment, she stared at her daughters and her heart warmed. It wasn't often they shared an intimate moment like now. Most of the time, Carol was annoyed with her younger sister, because Chloe could occasionally be a whiner. Quietly approaching them, she sat on the edge of the coffee table and watched them sleep. Carol's arms were wrapped tightly around Chloe and their foreheads were touching.

Focusing on Carol, she noticed her red-rimmed eyes and her damp cheeks.

She'd been crying. *Oh shit.* Was it the rumor she'd heard earlier from Lia and Julia that the girls weren't getting along? Had exchanged words even, and had argued…?

And the thing she'd apparently said that upset Ella? Was that it?

She had to bring that subject up with her soon…but right now, she was too tired.

Or…. Was it something else entirely?

There were days Carol seemed troubled and anxious over seemingly small things. But lately, she'd been abrupt and argumentative most of the time, generally where her girlfriends and boys were concerned. And admittedly, she was quick to throw darts at people and wedge her two cents into conversations.

Her girl loved to stir up trouble, tell secrets, and occasionally make up stories and downright lies. *What am I going to do with this child, who is almost a woman?*

Maggie brushed a thumb over her cheek.

Carol's eyes fluttered open, and they locked gazes.

"You okay?" Maggie whispered.

"Umhmm. Yeah."

"Hungry?"

"Yes."

"I brought food."

Her head bobbed. "Good. In a minute." Carol lazily sat up and stretched.

Maggie supposed Carol would not be forthcoming with any information about what caused her tears, so she would not ask. Yet.

Give it a few minutes.

"Okay. I'm going to take a quick shower and then put on my pajamas. We're in for the night, so get comfy."

"I'm good." Carol sat up a little. "Chloe ate a ton of popcorn, then two candy bars."

"And you let her?"

She shrugged and smiled. "She was having fun."

Maggie gave her a gentle smile, then smoothed a palm over Carol's head. "Thanks for taking care of her," she said softly. "You're a good sister. Now, go get some food."

Carol held her gaze for a moment, then smiled.

Jason bounded out of the bedroom, his hair dripping. "Is that food in the box?"

"Yes, it is."

"Great. I'm starved."

Maggie watched while her older two laid out the sandwiches and snacks, and she headed for the shower.

After dinner and an hour of television, she roused all three of them from the sofa and sent them off to bed. Carol and Chloe shared one bed, and Jason had the other. She tucked them in, watching their faces soften in sleep, and remembered the early days when they were so young. Time had marched on.

A few minutes later, she'd settled into bed herself and was nearly asleep when her door opened slightly, and a shaft of light penetrated the darkness. She'd left a lamp turned on beside the sofa.

"Mom. Are you awake?" Carol's voice was soft but a little shaky.

She sat up. "Yes, honey. What's wrong?"

"Can we talk? I need to tell you something."

Well, brace yourself, Maggie. Here it comes. "Then close that door to a crack and come here."

Carol climbed into bed and burrowed into Maggie's side, throwing her arms around her. Whatever was bothering her daughter was more than a stupid skirmish with the girls. Something was wrong.

"What is it, sweetie. You can tell me."

Carol let go of a breath. "It's big and it's going to hurt you, so I don't know exactly how to say it."

Oh shit. She's pregnant. Oh, fuck.

"It's about Dad."

"What?" That took her a little off guard.

"I talked to him after you left. His connection was open, and he was there, but he didn't know I was there."

Oh no. What did she see? "What did he say?"

Carol fell silent. Maggie waited.

"Mom, he wasn't alone. He was in bed with a woman. And there was a baby."

Maggie stayed quiet for a few minutes, the pang in her chest more for the hurt she felt in Carol's words, than for herself. She'd lost any love she'd had for Max years ago.

But hurt her children? No. She would not let that happen.

"Oh sweetheart..." she breathed.

"I don't understand it."

"Well, to be honest, there are some things you should probably know that would help you make sense of this. If that's possible."

"Like what? Did you know this? You don't seem upset."

"No. I didn't know... But honey, there have been others."

"Other women? Has there ever been a baby? I think it's his."

Those words stabbed her heart a bit and for the moment, she was glad for the darkness. They could simply talk and not worry about facial expressions and such.

"You're seventeen years old. It's time you know the truth about your father and me."

"What do you mean...the truth?"

Maggie sighed. "The truth you need to know about my marriage to your dad. Look, honey, I don't want you to end up like me. I don't want you to make the same mistakes."

"What do you mean?"

"Stuck in a situation you can't get out of."

"I don't understand, Mom. You don't want to be with Dad?"

Did she? How ironic that her child had to ask that question. Was Carol operating on some Pollyanna version of what a marriage should be? That they were happy? Surely, she'd seen Max's aggression, and listened to his belittling.

Exhaling, Maggie took another breath and waited for a round of thunder to pass. "Carol, when your dad and I married, I agreed to a rather untraditional type of marriage, called an open marriage. That means that we are, of course, legally married—but he still wanted to be able to see other women. The arrangement we made when I became pregnant with you was that he would work and provide the income, I would stay home and take care of the house and raise the children, but he still had his freedom."

"What about your freedom?"

Maggie touched her face. "See, you are already smarter than I was at that time. All I saw was that he was going to take care of me. I guess at the time I wanted that. But now...."

"Now he treats you like shit."

At the moment, Maggie almost wished she could see Carol's face. "You've noticed?" Was she more perceptive than she'd thought?

"Yes. Jason has too. Why do you let him do that, Mom?" She paused, then said, "Oh..."

The hint of realization was resolute in Carol's voice.

"Honey, I haven't worked for years, and I have no money to my name. According to your dad, he was the provider, and I didn't need money. Only what he gave me."

Which now, saying that out loud, made her realize how much control Max truly had over her. It wasn't just sex. It was money, too. And every other damn thing in their lives.

Including the children.

Carol sat up on an elbow. "So, in other words, he could fuck around but you couldn't. He controlled the money, and you had nothing unless he gave it to you."

"That's right."

"Could you fuck around too?"

Maggie gasped slightly at her daughter's candid words. "No. He preferred to keep me busy at home."

"But could you? Did you ever?"

She thought about the cowboy. "Once. Not long ago. But that's over."

"Did Dad know?"

"No."

"Why didn't you just tell him? Make sure he knew things were even."

Maggie paused the conversation, waiting for several seconds to roll by. Sounded simple, right? But not so much. "Because he would have beaten the shit out of me, Carol. He would have used it against me in so many ways. With you kids, with money, everything. At this point, after twenty years, he feels like I'm his property. He wants me home and in bed when he wants me, and that's about the extent of it."

Carol laid back down, the silence ticking on. "That sucks, Mom. I wondered once if he'd hit you. You had bruises."

"Yeah. It does suck." Maggie recalled the incident from last summer. "You remember when your dad and you showed up at Tequila Sunrise? That was because I told him I wanted a divorce."

"He was super angry at you."

"You were a bit annoyed with me too."

Carol huffed. "I was being a snotty child. I've grown up." She paused, then added. "Besides, I didn't know the whole story, so I should have stayed out of it. I'm sorry about that day, Mom. I was a brat."

Maggie smiled at that. Maybe in some ways she had grown up. In others, she had a long way to go.

"Yes, you were." She gathered Carol closer. "But that was then."

"Mom. So, are there other babies?"

A baby. She'd never once even considered that, knowing how angry Max was, every time she'd gotten pregnant. "I doubt if there are other babies. Frankly, I'm surprised about this one."

She would not—*and never would*—let her children know their father didn't want them. She also would never let them become pawns in their marriage game.

At all costs, she had to protect the kids.

Carol maintained the silence. "Do you think this time, with this woman, things are different?"

That was a good question. "I don't know sweetheart."

"But if it is different, and he loves her and has a baby with her, then what? Will you divorce? What happens to you? Us? Me and Jason and Chloe?"

Oh, fuck her brain went there way too quickly.

"Sweetheart, let's not imagine scenarios that may never come true. Okay?" She paused, waiting to see if Carol said anything more, then added, "Did your dad say anything about telling me?"

"He told me *not* to tell you. That he would talk to you."

"I see." *The bastard.*

"Did he try to call you?"

"No. He didn't."

With a crack of thunder and a bolt of lightning, the room suddenly lit up, then went totally black. The light in the living room flickered off, then on, then off again.

"We lost power." Carol nestled closer.

Maggie realized it wasn't only because of the storm. "You okay?" she asked. "This should be over by tomorrow night."

"The storm, you mean?"

"Yes."

The other crap would linger on for a long, long time, she was sure.

Outside, an updraft of wind abruptly rattled the bedroom window. A clap of thunder jarred the room. Carol burrowed closer into Maggie's side, wrapping her arms around her. Tight.

"I'm scared, Mom." Carol's voice was soft, barely audible.

"Me, too," Maggie whispered.

They weren't talking about the storm.

Jason and Chloe burst into the room then, slamming the door against the wall. Within seconds, they were in bed with her, too.

The light flickered back on, but dimmer than before.

Maggie whispered into Carol's ear. "No word to the littles, or anyone, until we know more. Okay?"

Carol nodded and wrapped her arms around her.

Ella & Alice

Eleven

Christmas Eve
Between 9 a.m. and Midnight

Ella McBain had had just about enough of Carol Oliver's snippy accusations. They'd argued throughout breakfast, and then the twit came out with this obvious lie about her mother being a lesbian. Frankly, what business of hers was it anyway, if she was?

"Stop! Just shut up about it. Okay? Stop talking."

Carol scoffed. "Fine. Look. Have a great day, girls. I'm off for an adventure."

"You better not go outside. The storm."

"Oh, what I have planned will definitely take place somewhere hot and steamy."

Ella rolled her eyes. "Use condoms, Maggie," she snarked.

"Quit mother henning me, Alice."

Carol sashayed across the restaurant, and Ella stood stone still watching her. The girl slowed while passing the fishermen's table, obviously ogling the younger man. She assumed that because the "hot guy" looked up and appeared to make eye contact as she passed.

113

Carol headed down the hall toward the restrooms.

"What a little slut."

Hannah stepped up beside her. "She's just trying to figure out life."

"Aren't we all?" She looked at Hannah. "Sorry about the drama. I know it's not what you wanted."

Hannah shrugged. "It is what it is."

"Do you think what she said is true?"

"I don't know, Ella. You know Carol better than me."

"She's a sneaky, bitchy mean girl."

"Well, then." Hannah sighed and scanned the room. "I'd take it all with a grain of salt."

But Ella wasn't sure she could, or if she should. Were there some grains of truth, rather than salt, to what Carol had said? Had her mother been hiding this from her? *What the hell?* And what about from her dad? That night she'd overheard them fighting, they'd said some things she didn't understand. Did that make sense now?

First, her parents never fought—at least within earshot of her—so that was extremely unusual. But they hadn't known she was home. She'd been out at the movies that evening with a friend and had come home early. They hadn't known when she'd slipped in the side door.

"Ella?"

"I'm sorry. What?"

"Thought I'd lost you there for a minute."

She shook her head. "Just thinking."

Glancing about, Hannah said, "You know, this place is pretty busy with everyone gathering in here. Do you want to talk? Maybe we can find a quiet place somewhere."

She wasn't sure she wanted, or needed, to talk. What would she say? She barely knew Hannah, anyway. "I should find my mother." She took a few steps.

"Wait." Hannah grasped her arm. "Hold up. Before you step into that conversation, let's chat a minute. Once you open that door, you can't close it again."

"So what? Are you an authority on the subject or something?"

"I have some experience."

"Well, I'm not sure I need advice right now, to be honest. I need to think."

"That's fair." Hannah met her gaze. "I'm betting your emotions are all balled up inside and you're not sure what you are feeling."

Ella hated to admit, even to herself, that Hannah was right. "I'm a mess on the inside."

"You could fool me by looking at you."

"I learned early in life not to show emotion—especially when I'm sad or confused or upset."

"Girl, we need to talk."

Hannah held her gaze, which made Ella a little uneasy.

"Let's get out of here."

Her head spun as Hannah took her hand and led her toward the exit. "I suppose I should get my feelings in check before I approach her."

"That's a good plan."

As they left the restaurant, a gust of chilly wind shoved them into the wall.

"Shit." Hannah grabbed her tighter. "That's some stiff breeze."

"This way," Ella said.

She'd been to the resort many times, so she was familiar with the layout. The inn was actually more like a long, three-story motel on stilts. The Sandcastle sat at the south end, angled in front of the hotel at sea-level. Even though tall dunes on the ocean side protected the lower level, the wind still whipped solidly through the pilings.

They left the restaurant by the rear door, and Ella hastily led her under the building. They rushed down the center and into the ground-level multipurpose room. She flipped the light switch.

Hannah glanced right and left. "This is where all the festive stuff happened last night."

"Yep. I figured no one would be here. Let's find a corner."

"How about over there where the kids were watching TV? There's a couch."

"Perfect."

They headed that way. "Looks like there's some cleaning up to do yet," Hannah said. "Maybe we should tidy up a little while we chat."

Ella exhaled and thought about that. It might be easier to talk while keeping her hands busy—she could avoid looking at Hannah directly that way. "Sure." She started picking up some scattered paper plates and cups.

Hannah did the same.

"Ella? A few minutes ago, you said you learned to hide your emotions early in life. Why is that?"

Why indeed?

Ella leaned over a table to pick up a few more paper plates and sighed. Her back was to Hannah. While thinking about her question, she found a large garbage can near the wall and deposited the trash she'd collected. "It's just a thing about my family," she said, not turning around.

"Oh?"

Hannah's response was definitely a prod for more information. *Am I ready to share more, though?* Shrugging, she turned. "In my family, being happy is a value. Being cheerful and upbeat is also valued. Being a sad-faced Debbie Downer is not."

"Ah." Hannah nodded. "I see."

"Do you? Really?"

"I get the concept," Hannah said.

Ella still faced her. "Do you realize what it's like having to always be perfect? Living in the same household with a teacher and a local government official? To uphold the family's expectations and reputation? Be an honor student. Look pretty. Be pleasant. Do good things. Don't swear. Keep your room clean. Don't kiss boys under the bleachers. Stay a virgin. *Shit.*" She turned away and spotted some more trash and stomped toward it. "And that's enough of that."

"Sounds like a lot of pressure."

Ella whirled back, locked her gaze with Hannah's, and gave her a broad smile. "No worries. I'm fine. I can handle it."

Nodding slowly, Hannah said, "Of course. Right."

"You don't believe me."

"Look. Full disclosure, here," Hannah said. "I'm in graduate school for social work, working on my master's degree in counseling. I'm also doing part-time therapy work for a local LGBTQ+ affirming group off campus. So, I have some skills. But I am not a licensed therapist yet...and I want you to know that I am *not* talking to you as a counselor or therapist. This is just you and me chatting as friends. Okay?"

"We're not friends." Ella stared at her, shaking her head. *Who is this chick anyway?*

"Of course." Taking a step, Hannah said calmly, "I just wanted that out in the open."

Ella inhaled deeply, then let the breath out with force. "I do not need a therapist or a counselor." Turning, she headed swiftly for the door. "I need to be alone. And then, when I've figured out some things in my head, I need to talk with my mother."

"That's good," Hannah offered.

"What?"

"You said 'talk *with* your mother' not 'talk *to* my mother.' Shows you want a two-sided conversation."

Whirling back after a few steps, she pinned Hannah with her gaze. "Don't analyze me. Don't tell me what's good. And don't follow me. I'm not in the mood to be preached to or taught things or counseled, particularly when I know my own mother, and I'm convinced what Carol said was a lie. I don't believe her. She was making things up."

"And what if she wasn't?"

What if...? What the hell if...? "Then I'll deal with it." Turning her back on Hannah, she pushed at the door. The wind caught and crashed it against the outside wall with a satisfying whack.

She blindly rushed for the stairs.

Shit. Shit. Shit! She never cursed—out loud or to herself. Why now? Did she feel like a rebel? Like the good girl gone wrong? Why *the fuck* had she always been so good, so pleasant? To please a mother who had been lying to her for years?

"Well, let's just find out," she muttered. Putting her head down against the wind, she climbed the stairs to the third floor and the suite she shared with her mother.

ALICE STRAIGHTENED AND CALLED OUT TO MAGGIE. GOD, her back hurt from all the sand shoveling. It would have helped if Ella had arrived to help, but so far, her daughter was AWOL.

"Alice?" Maggie rushed forward. "Goodness. You look exhausted."

"I am. It's only been about fifteen minutes of shoveling, but I'm not used to this kind of thing. Can you help me?"

"Sure. That's why I'm here." Maggie lifted the bag and opened it so Alice could shovel. "Wait. Here. Give me that shovel. I'll do that part. You hold."

Alice was only too happy to switch. "I swear, I need to get away from my desk more and exercise. I have no strength."

"You're busy working for the mayor. That's important stuff." Maggie tilted her shovel, and the sand dropped in—although the storm breeze had other ideas for about half of it. "Goodness, that wind is wicked."

"It's only going to get worse."

"That's what I was afraid of. Let's see how many of these we can get done."

Alice nodded. "The guys will come and get them with the truck. They've already taken the ones done earlier."

"I saw them from my window out at the cottages."

They continued shoveling for a few minutes, fighting the wind and updrafts of sand in their faces, and filled five bags.

Alice straightened. "Do you have any idea where the girls are?"

Maggie stopped shoveling and sighed, looking back. "Well, Carol was behind me when we left the room and was supposed to be helping but she's disappeared. Maybe they are together?"

"Maybe."

"Maybe they are even working together."

Alice glanced at the small crowd helping to shovel. "Unless they are boarding up windows, which I doubt, I think they've given us the slip."

Maggie rolled her eyes. "I can see that with Carol, but Ella? She's so responsible."

"Mom!"

Both women twisted to see Ella marching toward them. Alice recognized the confused look on her daughter's face. "Honey, are you okay? We were just talking about you and Carol."

"I don't want to talk about Carol." Ella planted herself squarely in front of Alice and gave Maggie a quick glance. "No. Things are not okay, Mom. And Maggie, I'm glad you are here to help clear up some things."

Panic squeezed Alice's heart, and a sharp pain took her breath. She exchanged a brief glance with Maggie, who had an *"oh shit"* look on her face.

"Goodness, Ella. What—"

"Are you gay, Mom?"

The question sucked every bit of breath from Alice's lungs. "Wh... Why would you ask that?"

Ella shifted her stance and scowled at Maggie. "Carol said you told her that mom was a lesbian. Is that true? Did you tell her that? And why would you do that? Because you know it's not true. She's been married to my dad for...what? Twenty-five years or more? She's obviously not gay."

Alice watched Maggie's mouth open and close as she stared, a little dumbfounded, at Ella. It wasn't often that Maggie didn't have anything to say, which surprised Alice. Somewhat. She grasped Ella's arm.

"Sweetheart. We need to talk."

Ella jerked her arm away. "I asked Maggie a question." She darted a look back at Maggie.

"I, uh. No. I didn't tell Carol anything like that." Maggie met Alice's gaze.

"So, she lied? That mean little snit. Why would she? Why would she make up something like that?"

A breath whooshed out of Maggie's mouth. "Ella. I don't know why she said what she did, but I didn't tell her anything about it."

Alice interrupted. "But could she have overheard us talking on the phone?"

Maggie abruptly met her gaze. "Oh, shit."

Ella whirled back and faced her. "So, it's true?" Her voice grew steadily louder. "It's true that you're gay? What the hell, Mom! Why didn't you tell me? How could you do this to Dad? All this time we've been living a lie?"

"Sweetheart, I didn't *do* anything to your dad. Being gay is not something you *do*. Life was different when your dad and I got married. Times were different. I didn't even really know how I felt about my sexuality back then. Over time...."

"Oh, hell. It's true."

"Ella, let's talk. Just you and me."

"No!" Her daughter backed away. "Is this why you and Dad are getting a divorce? *Oh. My. God.* Have you been humping other women on the side and Dad didn't even know? *Does* he know? I can't believe you've lied all these years." She took another step backward.

"Woman."

"What?"

"Woman. Not women. I've only been with one woman, and you might as well know that I love her."

"Who?"

Alice sucked in a breath and simultaneously, her lower lip. "I can't tell you that."

"Shit." Ella took a few steps and paced in a circle. "Shit. Shit. Shit. What else are you not telling me?"

Alice tried to stop Ella's pacing by grasping her shoulders. "Sweetheart...."

Ella shrugged her off. "Don't touch me. I don't know you anymore."

Maggie moved in beside Alice, wrapping an arm around her shoulder. "Ella, being a lesbian isn't a bad thing. Your mom just realized later in life and...."

Swinging toward Maggie, Ella scoffed. "Oh God. Spare me. I've already heard that argument from Hannah."

Her words surprised Alice. *Hannah?* "Why, Hannah?"

"Probably because she's older, more mature, and college educated?" Maggie shared. "I'm sure she's very open-minded and liberal."

"Hell, she's gay too. Maybe you two should compare notes."

Alice and Maggie shared a look.

"Ella...."

"I'm going to call Dad." Alice watched her daughter stomp away, then twist back. "He knows. Right?"

Alice nodded.

"Great. Just great. Everyone knew but me."

"Honey, it wasn't the right time."

Ella glared. "Well, the time found me whether it was right or not, thanks to Carol."

"I'm so sorry," Maggie whispered in Alice's ear, tightening her hug.

"I'm leaving." Ella shouted. "I have my keys. I'm going to the cabin."

Alice bolted forward. "No! The storm!"

Ella glanced back. "Oh, you care? Right."

"Let her go," Maggie said. "She's heading inland. She will be okay. Maybe safer."

Ella darted out from under the hotel and into the parking lot. Alice watched her rush off into the stormy mist. Her heart sank heavily in her chest, constricting her breathing, her head pounding. An outburst of wind and sand and rain raced through the pilings and whipped around them. Alice's tears mingled with the salt mist streaking her face.

"Come on," Maggie said softly. "Let's get inside."

Exhausted, she slanted into Maggie's embrace.

Who would have thought? Me leaning on Maggie?

ELLA DIDN'T HAVE THE KEY FOB ON HER KEY RING TO OPEN the door remotely and struggled to get the key in the lock. The pelting rain and wind didn't help. When she finally unlocked the car and plopped into the driver's seat, slamming the door and relocking it behind her, the tears came.

And it wasn't a pretty cry.

For several minutes, she let loose with an uncontrollable round of sobbing, complete with hiccups and steering wheel pounding and occasional swearing.

"Fuck. Fuck. Fuck!"

A long breath whooshed from her lungs as the sobs subsided and she sat, looking out the windshield. She stilled for a moment, thinking, then picked up her phone and called her dad.

It rang three times, then went to voice mail. That wasn't unusual. Generally, the cell phone service at the cabin was spotty. He usually retrieved his messages when he went down the hill to the general store.

She left a voice mail. "Dad, I'm on my way to the cabin to spend Christmas with you. I'll see you in a few hours."

Maybe I should stop by the house first and get some dry clothes.

After plugging her phone into the car charger, she started the engine and, with a sigh of relief, headed away from the stormy madness of Tuckaway Bay, and all the little storms inside Sea Glass Inn.

"Whew. Thank goodness."

Twelve

Maggie: *Alice's room. 315. STAT!*
Julia: *What's going on?*
Maggie: *Trouble*
Julia: *Shit. What now?*
Maggie: *Tell you in a few.*
Julia: *We're settling into our suite. Give me 5*
Lia: *What did I miss?*
Maggie: *It's Ella...and Carol. Alice.*
Maggie: *Just get to Alice's suite!*
Julia: *Fuck. Girls OK? Alice?*
Maggie: *Questionable....*
Lia: *Alice???*
Maggie: *5 minutes. Just get here. ASAP*

ALICE WATCHED THE MESSAGES FLY INTO HER MESSENGER
app. She didn't respond. Couldn't. No way could she process what had
just happened with Ella, and appropriately reply to her girlfriends
simultaneously.

She'd wait until they all got to her suite.

Maggie took the key card from her hand, swiped the door lock, then led Alice into the main room. On impulse, Alice jogged to the bedroom she shared with Ella and looked around for her things.

"She didn't take anything with her! All her stuff is still here." Immediately, she burst into tears—something she hadn't wanted to do and tried to hide from Maggie. "Shit." She rubbed her eyes.

"She was upset," Maggie said. "Does she have things at the cabin?"

She faced her. "Yes. Of course." Glancing about the room, she was both upset and sad at seeing all of Ella's things strewn about. Sniffling, she purposely didn't look at Maggie. For as perfect as her daughter was most of the time, she could be terribly messy at others.

"Here." Maggie picked up a couple of articles of clothes from the floor. "Let's tidy up."

"No!" Alice snatched the T-shirt and jeans from Maggie's hands. "Just leave it. Makes me feel like she's here."

Maggie sighed so loud Alice could hear her frustration. "Fine."

"Sorry. Didn't mean to be snippy."

"Not a problem, Alice. You're allowed to be snippy, woman! It's been a day already, and it's not over."

Crossing her arms over her chest, to keep herself together than anything else, Alice stomped off toward the bedroom window, swiped at her face, paced back toward Maggie, then to the window again. She peered out at the brewing storm.

"It's okay to be upset, honey. Cry if you want. Even perfect people cry."

Well, I don't. At least not in front of people.

"The storm will ease up...eventually."

"It's awful out there. Oh, my poor girl."

"Remember, she's driving inland."

"But just a couple of hours!" She whirled back and paced some more. "You know how the mountains often get as much rain as the coast at times, and flooding can be worse! Those creeks and the low places...."

"Alice..." Maggie grasped her arm, stopping her pacing. "Get a grip. Stop overthinking."

"I need to call George."

"Good idea."

Alice fumbled for her phone in her pocket. It wasn't there. "Shit. Where is my phone? Did I leave it somewhere?"

"Did you take it out to the sandbags?"

Slightly panicking, she glanced about the room, spotting the thing on the nightstand. "No. There it is."

Maggie retrieved it and handed it over. "Call him so he will be waiting for her."

"Maybe he could meet her at the store."

"Great idea."

"Then he can call me back."

"Yes."

Alice pressed George's name on her call list and waited. Three rings. No answer. She left a message. "George. Call me ASAP."

He would, she knew. He never *didn't* call her back when she left an ASAP message.

"Let's go sit." Maggie led her out of the bedroom.

Alice dropped into a soft overstuffed chair. Numb, she faced the sliding glass doors to the deck, and the storm. While she was anxious, she also felt frozen and detached. Just going through the motions, letting Maggie lead her around and tell her what to do.

What the hell? I should be taking charge and getting my girl back!

A series of loud knocks came at the door. "Alice!"

Maggie rushed that way. Julia and Lia tumbled inside, their fists raised as if about to knock again. They took one look at Alice and halted.

"Oh crap. Are you *crying*? You never cry," Julia said, rushing toward her.

"I must look like hell."

"What the fuck, Alice?" Julia crouched in front of her.

Parking herself on the arm of Alice's chair, Lia met Maggie's gaze. "She *is* crying! What happened?"

"Tell them, Maggie," Alice blurted out.

Maggie bit her lip. "I'm afraid it's all my fault."

Julia stood. "Why?"

"Carol told Ella that Alice is gay."

"What?"

Alice registered the shocked look on Julia's face.

"How did Carol know?" Julia asked.

"I don't know. Maybe she overheard us discussing on the phone," Maggie said. "I did not tell her directly. Why would I?"

"Could she have read your text messages?"

Maggie shook her head. "I keep my phone locked up tight."

Alice interrupted. "Ella said something about her and Carol arguing at breakfast."

"Oh, dear." Julia glanced off. "Hannah got back to the room right before I left. I asked her where she'd been, and she said that she and Ella were talking. I wonder if she knows more?"

"Can you text her? Maybe she can tell us what went down."

"I'll call Sam. I don't have her number. Give me a second." Julia sauntered off to the bedroom.

"Well, let's hope Carol wasn't exaggerating and mean about it."

Maggie slanted her gaze at Lia. "What do you mean?"

Blinking rapidly, Lia stood and faced Maggie. "Well, you know...right?"

Alice reached for Lia's hand, sensing some rising tension. That's the last thing she needed—her friends arguing too, right now.

"Maggie, you know I don't say much, but Carol can push buttons and wildly exaggerate at times."

"I've already told Alice I'm sorry."

"But how did Carol know in the first place?" Lia stepped closer. "I mean, surely you didn't tell her."

"I did not!"

Oh dear. Alice shifted in her seat. "Ladies. Stop."

Julia burst into the room. "I have some info."

They all turned toward her.

"Great," Maggie said, eyeing Lia.

"What did Hannah say?" Alice prodded.

"Well, according to Sam, who got the deets from Hannah, who evidently witnessed the entire thing..." Julia hesitated, briefly. "Carol and Ella *and* Belle all had words this morning."

"About...?"

"What we thought... Carol told Ella that Alice was a lesbian. I guess they tossed a few zingers back and forth about both Alice and Maggie before that."

"Zingers? Like what?"

Julia huffed out a hard breath. "Well, basically, one of those... You know, *your mother said, my mother said* things...."

Alice stood. "Go on, Julia. You're not telling it all."

"Shit, Alice. They argued. Can we leave it at that?"

"No, we can't." Maggie approached Julia. "Tell us the rest."

"Jesus, you both are persistent." Julia took a breath. "Alright. Apparently, Ella kept saying Carol was acting like her mother, and Carol told Ella that Maggie always makes fun of Alice behind her back, calling her boring and a goody-two-shoes, and Ella said that was better than screwing men in pickup trucks like Maggie does, and Carol basically said that was better than humping women like Alice does."

A prolonged pause settled over the room.

"Well, shit." Maggie walked off toward the deck door.

Alice turned to Julia. "By the way, did you know Hannah is gay?"

Julia stood stone still, staring.

"I guess not."

"Sorry, that took me by surprise," Julia said.

Maggie added, "Apparently, she tried to counsel Ella, which is kind of sweet when you think about it. Do you think Sam knows?"

Julia shook her head. "I have no clue if he does, but no... He's never indicated. Wow."

"It will be fine," Alice said. "She's young and has already found her way."

"Oh, I'm not concerned about that. I'm totally fine with however Hannah lives her life. Sam is another story."

"Will you tell him?"

"Oh, *hell* no!" Julia shouted. "That's Hannah's story to tell."

Alice almost giggled at Julia's expression, and it was a bit of relief to let go of the drama, even for only a few seconds. Then she thought of something. "I'm just curious. Lia. Have you talked to Belle in the past couple of hours?"

"She's still with her dad, so no."

Julia intercepted. "I wondered about that. Hannah said Carol and Belle had words too, and that Belle left before the Maggie-Alice argument."

"Well then, it sounds like Carol was the shit stirrer," Lia said.

Alice watched Maggie's body twist back as she faced them all. "Well, of course she is! She's a little bitch. And apparently, just like her mother. Is that what you all think of me, too?"

Stunned, Alice just stood there, watching Maggie's facial expressions contort between anger and distress.

"Do you all talk about me behind my back?" Maggie pushed.

Stepping toward her, Alice said, "No more than you all talk about me, apparently." She reached for Maggie's arm. "Hey, look. We're all acting a little perimenopausal, so let's...."

Maggie jerked her arm away. "Don't. I'm just upset. I'm not old enough to be menopausal."

"Peri," Julia interjected. "Perimenopausal, and yes, we all are old enough."

"Shit. I don't need that, too," Maggie wailed.

Lia rushed forward, glancing at all of them. "Stop. Look. We're all a little distraught. Let's not let this come between us. Right now, we need to focus on the girls."

"Yes." Alice stepped back. "Oh, Ella...."

"That's the problem," Maggie said. "The big thing we haven't said yet." She looked at Julia and Lia. "Ella took Alice's car and left."

"What? In this storm?" Julia took a step. "Where did she go?"

"To the cabin."

"Call George!"

"I tried. No service."

"Shit."

"Should we go after her?" Lia asked.

Alice shook her head. "No. I let her go. She was upset and angry and thinks I've lied to her for years, that I was unfair to George, and frankly, she wants nothing to do with me right now. So, I let her go."

Maggie nodded. "I keep telling her she's heading inland, away from the storm, so she will be okay once she gets off the island."

"I'm sure George will call you as soon as he can," Lia said.

Alice nodded. "Of course."

But she wasn't feeling optimistic. Her scattered brain couldn't control her thoughts of things that could go wrong, and her heart felt like mincemeat, chopped up into tiny bits and shredded. She looked at her friends.

"It's going to be a long few hours until I know she is safe."

"We're here, Alice."

She shook her head. "You all have families to take care of. I'm fine."

"No, we're staying," Maggie insisted.

That's when Alice decided and said firmly. "To be honest, I want to be alone. I appreciate your being here right now, but I need to process what has happened and figure out how to move forward. You all understand?"

"Alice, you don't have to make any decisions now." Lia leaned closer.

"No, I don't. But I need to think this through and right now, I just want to be alone."

The three of them stood there for a long moment. The quiet in the room strangely outweighed the heaviness of the storm outside.

Maggie gave her a hug and kissed her cheek. "You know where we are if you need us."

Nodding, she said, "I do."

Lia grasped her hand and smiled.

Julia gave her a hug.

They left. And Alice was alone with the consequences of her actions. Or perhaps, her inactions.

***

THE STORM WAS RELENTLESS, AND POWERFUL.

Once she'd crossed the bridge to the mainland, the winds had subsided somewhat, but the rain still kept coming down in droves. As she continued west and north toward the mountains, things changed. The wind blew hard, rain slanting into her windshield, making it difficult to see even with her wipers going full blast. Gusts of wind shook the car, threatening to shoot her off the highway. Heavy black clouds hung low against the mountains and occasionally, a clap of thunder and a wicked streak of lightning raced crankily over them.

She was moving slower than she usually drove, but it was like the storm had stood still. Like it had nestled itself against the foothills and wasn't budging.

Ella debated going on.

Or returning home.

Perhaps she should go back home to their house on Tuckaway Bay. She'd left there an hour ago, after she'd showered, changed her clothes, and gathered a few things. No way would she go back to the resort...but maybe she'd be safer heading back home?

She wasn't making good time. At all. The storm was severely slowing her down. She had at least a couple of hours to go.

On impulse, she turned on a local radio station. "Maybe I can get local storm news."

All she got was static.

Simultaneously, a weather alert sounded on her phone. Slowing, and checking her rearview mirror for traffic behind her—there was none—she picked up the phone and read the alert.

Severe weather imminent. Coastal and mountain regions of eastern North Carolina. High winds. Record rainfall. High tides. Possible threat of tornados and flooding. Watch for icy patches on roads as temperatures drop. Emergency vehicles only recommended on roadways.

"Great."

She needed to find an exit or turnoff and head back to Tuckaway Bay. It appeared there was one coming up, not too far down the road. The storm squall pushed at the car, rain pelting the windshield. Fortunately, she could still see. She'd feel safer if she could get off this highway and find some smaller roads... Or maybe, for a while, some kind of overhead shelter to park under until this blowing wind passed.

Suddenly, the car sputtered, lurched, and slowed... And she wasn't braking.

"What the...?"

She glanced at the gas gage. *Empty.*

The car stalled.

Hannah, Sam, & Julia

Thirteen

CHRISTMAS EVE
Between 9 a.m. and Midnight

HANNAH WATTERS WAS THE KID ALWAYS STICKING HER NOSE in other people's business.

It wasn't because she wanted to hurt someone, or be a tattletale, or a know-it-all. It was because she wanted to help people. From the time she was a very little girl, she knew that when she grew up, she would either be a teacher or a doctor, or some other helper person.

In fact, when she was in the second grade, Mrs. Smitz, the principal of her elementary school, visited her classroom one day and asked all the children what they wanted to be when they grew up. Most of her classmates said things like firefighter, or football player, or singer, or nurse. Hannah said she wanted to be a helper.

The expression on Mrs. Smitz's face was rather odd, Hannah had thought then, but she'd never forgotten it. Her look was a cross between amusement and surprise and compassion. That's when Mrs. Smitz invited her to be her office helper for thirty minutes every day. The principal would write notes to teachers, put them in an envelope with the teacher's name and classroom number on them, and Hannah would stop in after lunch to pick them up and deliver.

She missed the after-lunch recess, but she didn't care.

Delivering them made her feel good, helping out—and Mrs. Smitz always seemed so appreciative.

Hannah supposed there weren't a lot of seven-year-olds who didn't put themselves first but were always thinking of others.

But that was who Hannah was then, as well as now.

Sometimes it was to her advantage, and other times, to her detriment.

During her fourth-grade year, Hannah was scolded more than once for helping her classmates with their work—and for finishing their sentences during read-aloud time, when the other kids couldn't figure out the next word.

Hannah knew the word, so why not tell them and help? They'd probably remember it the next time, anyway. Right?

But her reading teacher didn't think so, and Hannah's mom always heard about it during parent-teacher conferences. And the words, "Hannah needs to keep her eyes on her own work," often showed up on her report cards. At first, her mom thought she'd been cheating, looking at other students' papers to get the answers. Then, she realized Hannah was giving the answers to the other students who were struggling.

Her mom told her she was proud of her for wanting to help—but that she had to stop and why.

That's when Hannah learned that helping had limits.

After fourth grade, she'd learned to be a bit more covert. In high school, it was easier. Because she was "the smart girl" her notebooks were always in high demand. She'd let people borrow her stuff during study hall—until her AP English teacher caught on.

Copying and plagiarism are not allowed.

"But I gave it away freely," she said to Mr. Garner, the high school assistant principal. "I could have charged them for it and made some cash on the side, but I didn't. I just wanted to help."

And he believed her. She still got detention.

Her mother, however, wasn't so pleased with the helping any longer, and reminded her about setting boundaries.

Hmm. Had she crossed a line with Ella today?

Maybe. Probably.

"So, Ella, my apologies for being the over-helpful new girl. It's just who I am. But of course, you don't know that because, you're right, we're not friends."

But she was speaking to the open door of the multipurpose room—Ella had left several minutes earlier, and Hannah had been standing there musing about her misunderstood helpfulness for the past several minutes. And now, the rain was slanting in the door and pooling on the tile floor. She supposed she should shut it, find a mop, and clean up the water.

She did. And two hours later, the entire multipurpose room was spic-and-span clean.

Smiling, she glanced back as she shut off the light and exited the space.

Helpful, indeed!

***

Until Thanksgiving, when they'd spent a long weekend together, Sam Watters had had very little relationship experience with his grown daughter. They'd made some headway over that November holiday, which pleased him to no end. This Christmas holiday, he hoped to work more on creating a deeper relationship with Hannah.

Oh, he'd tried in the past, when she was younger. Somehow, it was easier to ply her with ice cream cones and movies when she was eight. But by the time she'd reached her young teenage years, treats and movies with dad weren't cutting it. And now that she was a college-educated woman, he was pretty damned sure they wouldn't work at this point, either.

He had to find some common ground.

Thing was, he had no clue where to start—so maybe he'd do what he'd always done. Let her take the lead.

Hannah spent her life with her mother in Albuquerque, New Mexico, while he'd been off serving his country. While that wasn't a bad thing—in fact, he was proud of his service—it drove a wedge into the relationship he'd had with Hannah's mother, and subsequently, with his daughter.

Now that Hannah was an adult, he was trying to remedy that. Julia had helped to push him forward. Last summer she had asked him, *What's Hannah's major in college? What's her favorite food? What books does she like to read?*

He couldn't answer because he wasn't sure.

"Well, isn't it about time you ask her? Just have a conversation with her, Sam. An adult conversation."

She was right. After all, he wasn't getting any younger.

Julia moved into the room and his gaze settled on her.

"I think we're set now. Should I put Hannah's things away?"

Sam shrugged. "I don't know. Let's wait and see. She may want to do that."

"I'm sure if I were a twenty-one-year-old woman, I wouldn't want a stranger rummaging around in my things."

"You're not a total stranger. We had a nice Thanksgiving."

"Yes, but we're not at the chummy stage yet, either. We barely know each other."

"This week will help."

"Yes, I suppose."

"Are you okay, Julia?"

Her expression was one of concern, and he wondered if he was pushing things between the two women in his life. The thing was, he and Julia still had so much to learn about each other, too. Their own relationship was just months old.

Julia smiled. "I'm fine. But if I get in the way, if you need time alone with your daughter, tell me. I can disappear for a while. I'm sure my girl-friends won't mind company."

Had she read his mind? "I will, honey."

"I'm just glad she hadn't unpacked much yet—it was easier to move her stuff from the cottage."

"I'm glad Zach had another suite he could offer us."

"Otherwise, we may as well have gone back home."

Sam grinned and grasped her around the waist, tugging her closer. "I like it when you call my place home."

She smiled, and he kissed the tip of her nose. He relished the contented sigh that escaped her lips.

"I do love you, Fisherman."

"And I you, College Girl."

They laughed at the pet names they'd established for each other early on.

The door to the suite pushed inward. Sam and Julia drifted apart.

"Hi sweetheart," Sam said.

"Hey. Zach told me we were in this suite number and gave me a key." Hannah looked them over. "Am I interrupting something?"

"Of course not." Julia smiled and stepped toward her. "We moved your things. Your bedroom is this way."

"Okay," Hannah said. "I wondered. Sorry I didn't get back to help you move."

"It only took a few minutes. Lia sent housekeeping over."

"At least now we're not at ground level."

"True."

Sam listened to the chitchat between his daughter and girlfriend. He wanted them to get along, to get to know each other too—but was that an unrealistic expectation for this weekend? There was so much going on, it seemed, with the storm, and all the people....

"Been spending some time with the girls, Hannah?"

She swung back and looked at him. "A little. Ella and I were just chatting downstairs. Then she... Well, she had to leave, so I finished cleaning the multipurpose room."

"You cleaned it?"

"Just tidied it up a little."

Sam grinned. He remembered that about his daughter. "You always did like keeping things neat and orderly."

"Just trying to be helpful."

Someone's phone pinged.

Julia pulled hers from her yoga pants pocket on her thigh. "Oh. Shit. I have to go." She looked at Sam, her fingers flying over the keyboard. "It's the girls. Do you mind?"

"Of course not." *That will give me some alone time with Hannah.*

"Great." She kissed him quickly on the lips. "I'll see you later."

Sam wondered what was going on. "Everything okay?"

She glanced at her phone again. More notifications were coming in. "Looks like something is going on with Ella and Alice. Maybe Carol, too. It's one of those ASAP texts, so... Gotta go."

"Oh shit is right," Hannah said.

Julia halted. "You know something."

"I do. Yes. But go. Better see what's going on. Alice may need you."

Sam caught and held Julia's stare for a moment, then she rotated toward the door and left. Sam switched gears and studied his daughter.

Hannah's face smacked of concern.

"You know what that was about?"

"Yeah. This may not be good." Hannah held her father's gaze.

Parking his fists on his hips, Sam squared himself. "Want to tell me?"

She shouldn't. Telling her dad wouldn't be helpful. Men just don't get things like what happened earlier, and she wasn't sure how he would react. And besides, how would his knowing be helpful? She didn't want to lie or get into the details.

She also didn't know what, if anything, he knew about Alice.

"Well, the thing is, at breakfast, some of the girls got a little huffy about some things and it sort of went south." There. That was all she was going to say.

"About...?" Her dad glared. He didn't look mean, just serious. Intense.

"Is that your Navy SEAL look?" Hannah asked, then grinned.

Her dad's face broke into a smile, too, and he relaxed. "Maybe." He took her hand. "Come over here. Let's sit for a while and chat."

"Sure, Dad."

"You're not going to tell me what happened, are you?"

They sat side-by-side on the sofa. The wind rattled the glass door.

"You wouldn't understand."

"I wouldn't?"

"It's a girl thing. You know. A hot guy. Everyone cooped up in the restaurant. Girl talk getting out of hand... That sort of thing."

Sam studied her. "There's a hot guy here?"

Hannah laughed. "Well, according to Carol, there is. One of the fishermen. The young one."

"Ah. That one."

"Yeah."

"So, it's a girl thing."

Hannah nodded. "Definitely a girl thing."

"Alrighty then." Sam paused, glancing about the room. Finally, he blurted out, "Want to watch a movie?"

Hannah thought about that for a couple of seconds. "Yes! An old one. Like something we used to go to the theater and watch when I was a kid."

A broad smile raced over her dad's face. Her heart lifted a little too. She realized she really loved that smile and liked it when he was happy.

Because it made her happy, too.

"The old Ghostbusters?"

"Perfect." She picked up the remote control and handed it to him. "Here, you work this thing and find it. I never know how these silly devices work."

He gave her a lingering glance, then turned toward the TV and fiddled with the remote.

Settling back against the sofa pillows, she leaned a little closer.

Her dad's phone rang then. He looked at it and said, "It's Julia. Do you mind?"

"Of course not. She might have news."

He paused the movie, and then tossed her a questioning glance while answering. "Hi, honey." He listened for a moment, and Hannah watched his facial expressions. After a few seconds, he turned and looked at her. "Hold on," he said to Julia.

Here it comes. "Dad?"

"Apparently, Alice is very upset after a fight she had with Ella. Seems Carol was involved. Can you give us more info about what happened between Carol and Ella earlier? It wasn't just a girl thing about a hot guy. Was it?"

Hannah blew out a sigh. "No. It wasn't." Something else must have happened, and it must be important, or Julia wouldn't have asked. She supposed it was time to talk. "Yes. You see, in a nutshell, the story is this. Carol told Ella that her mother is a lesbian."

Sam blinked. "That Maggie is a lesbian? Oh, darlin' that doesn't make sense."

"No, no." Hannah shook her head. "Carol told Ella that Alice is a lesbian."

"Well, we all knew that. I mean, Julia and her friends. And of course, Julia told me. I don't think it's well known in the community but—"

Hannah held up a hand. "Dad. Ella didn't know. She freaked out."

"Oh." He nodded. "Shit."

"Yeah. That's why I was talking to her earlier. Kind of giving her some advice."

One of her dad's brows arched. The one over his right eye. "Oh?"

Shit. Now or never. The door is open, Hannah. "Yeah. Dad. I have some experience with being gay, so I shared a few things."

Her dad blinked a few times again, more rapidly this time. The brow remained peaked. "You have experience being—"

"I work in therapy, Dad," Hannah interrupted. "I volunteer for an LGBTQ+ affirming group in Santa Fe twice a week. It's part of my graduate school program."

"Graduate school. Right." Sam thought for a minute. "Hannah, what is your major again? Have I ever asked you that?"

Smiling, she reached for her dad's hand, weaving her fingers with his. "My BS is in social work. I'm in graduate school for psychology. I want to focus on LGBTQ+ issues."

"Because you're gay."

"I am." Slowly, Hannah nodded. "Yes. I'm gay, Dad. I'm a lesbian. I came out years ago, before college. Mom has always known, or so she says. I just didn't know how to tell you. I was hoping to, soon."

"Well." His eyes closed then, his brow relaxed, and he reached for her. "Sweetheart, come here." He gathered her into his arms and held her close. "I love you. I hope you know that by now. The only thing I wish for you is love—however it comes to you."

Tears stung the backs of her eyelids as she drew back and studied her father's face. Why had she been so nervous about telling him? "You know what's the best thing about me being a lesbian?"

One corner of Sam's mouth drew up into a grin. "No, what?"

"You're the only man in my life. Forever."

Julia stepped into the suite and silently tiptoed across the room to turn down the sound on the TV. Seemed the movie Ghostbusters was ending, but no one was awake to watch it.

Glancing toward the sofa, she studied Sam and Hannah there. The remote control dangled from Sam's fingers. Smiling to herself, she'd observed that scenario many times since she'd moved in with him. Had they ever watched a complete movie together without him falling asleep?

She thought not.

But the thing that was different was Hannah, who was sleeping against his shoulder. Sam had wrapped an arm around her, and her head had fallen softly into the crook of his shoulder and chest. Both were breathing gently and evenly, looking very comfortable with each other.

Julia couldn't help but smile. Suddenly, she was glad she'd had a reason to slip away for an hour. Even if that hour was messy.

Carefully, she lifted the remote control from Sam's fingertips and set it aside.

She ambled off to her bedroom, used the bathroom, and then lay on her bed. While the storm still shook the windows and deck rails, she felt safe with Sam in the next room. And content. She was so glad that Sam and Hannah were spending time together and getting along—at least, that's how it appeared.

She thought about what she'd learned earlier—about Hannah being gay. While that was a non-issue for her, her views were liberal on the subject, and she hated when any person was forced to be different than they were, or wanted to be—but worried slightly how Sam might take it.

Knowing him, and how loving he could be, she assumed he would take it all in stride.

However, he was also a somewhat conservative-thinking military man, and she really didn't know his views on the subject—they had never deeply discussed either of their political beliefs.

Perhaps a conversational subject to approach after the holidays.

No way would she bring it up now. Nor would she bring up that Hannah was possibly gay. After all, it was hearsay at this point.

Unless she'd already told him—in the past hour or so.

And that was Hannah's business.

While her time with Sam had been relatively short—since August—the two of them had created a bond she knew would last forever. Knew it in her heart and deep in her soul. Interfering in any business between Sam and Hannah was not in her best interest. Or anyone's. She planned to be with Sam for a very long time.

Longer than long, even.

There was no place else she wanted to be than with him.

Not Louisville.

Not the B&B.

And definitely not in the world of corporate law.

No. All she wanted was Sam, their cozy beach house, fishing, cooking him breakfast and dinner, and living their lives together.

A sudden crash against the large window in her room jarred her thoughts and frightened her into an upright position. "Sam!"

He yelled from the living room. "Julia!"

Within seconds, he was at her side. "Are you okay?"

"I'm fine." Suddenly, water was spurting toward them, rolling down the inside of the window. "Is the glass cracked?"

Hannah rushed into the room, too. "It was a beach chair from the patio below. It's now on the deck. A big wooden one. Oh shit, the window is broken!"

Sam paced back and forth. "We can't sleep in this room tonight. Let's gather some bedding and our stuff and camp out in the living room."

"You can have my room," Hannah said. "I can sleep on the sofa. I think it's a pullout."

Sam nodded. "Let's figure that out in a minute. Can you two clear out this room? I'm going downstairs to get Zach and hopefully some supplies to board up that window from the inside." He paused for a moment, staring at the cracked glass. "I can't believe the wind lifted a chair that heavy and tossed it all the way up here."

"The winds are picking up, I guess," Hannah said. "I had just woken up when I saw it."

"Well, let's get moving." Sam headed out of the room.

"We're on it," Julia said.

The next second, he was gone.

Julia stared at Hannah. "It's okay. We'll be fine."

"I know." She nodded. "Dad will see to that."

"Yes."

They both just stood there, looking at each other.

"I'm a little scared," Hannah added. "Are you?"

Jula took two steps and wrapped her arms around Hannah in a motherly way. "I am."

They stood there for a moment in an embrace. Julia could feel Hannah's heart pounding against her chest. She gave her another squeeze, her own chest tightening and her breathing growing shallow.

"Let's get that stuff together," Hannah murmured after a minute.

They separated and went about gathering blankets and pillows, tossing them on the chairs and sofa in the living room. A few minutes later, Sam burst back into the room.

He looked at them both and heaved a quick, troublesome sigh.

"Grab what you can, what you think you will need for the night. Pillows. Blankets. Phones and charging cords. We're headed downstairs.

"Why?" Julia wasn't prone to panic. She'd been trained not to. But at the moment, her panic button was working overtime.

"We're all sheltering in place in the Sandcastle."

"All?" Suddenly, she was more than frightened.

Hannah reached for her hand. Julia squeezed it back.

"Yes. Everyone. Zach's orders."

Belle

Fifteen

CHRISTMAS EVE
Between 11 a.m. and....

HE'D KNOWN ALL THIS TIME AND HADN'T SAID A WORD.

Her dad sat back in the restaurant booth and sighed. "Just waiting for you, sweetheart. Now, tell me you are okay, and fill me in on the details."

A breath whooshed from between Belle's lips. "I guess since you've spoken with Dr. Speakman, you know that my heart is okay, and they are not concerned about my health? They expect a normal birth."

Grant nodded. "That's what he said. And realize, please, that the only reason he could talk to me about this is that I'm still listed as a person who can get your medical information on your forms."

"I didn't even consider that. I don't mind, Dad. I just wanted to be the one to share the news."

"So, tell me more. Who is the lucky father?"

Lucky. Right. One night stand lucky.... "Well, that's a long story. Or maybe a short one, depending on how you look at it. The short version is that it was once, and he doesn't know."

He eyed her. Belle felt a little uncomfortable.

Luna and Ginger stayed silent.

"That doesn't sound like you. Care to share the long version?"

Not really.

But she should. In fact, if she got it all out now, maybe she wouldn't have to repeat it. "It's really not that much longer, to be honest. It was a fling. He was a vacationer. I got carried away. *We* got carried away. He was gone Monday morning."

"Have you spoken with him?"

She shook her head. "No. He said he'd call. He didn't."

"Did you try to get in touch with him?"

"I did. I called his sister, who he was staying with here, because we have the records. She wasn't cooperative and told me not to call back."

His face froze, and Belle knew he likely had some choice words for the young man who had knocked up his daughter. "He doesn't know he's going to be a father?"

Please don't pull a Hannah on me, Dad. Not now. The day has already been trying enough. "No, he doesn't. His lack of communication tells me enough to know he's not interested in me, so… I'm sure he's not interested in a child. I'll not force him to be a father if he doesn't want to be."

"He's a father, no matter what."

"Biologically speaking. True. And if in the future he steps forward, I will tell him, and then he has some decisions to make—namely to decide if he wants to be part of his child's life. In the meantime, my baby has a mother and a loving family."

Jenn approached the table then, smiling. "Good morning! At least it's still morning for a few more minutes. What can I get everyone to drink? Coffee?"

"Yes, please," Ginger said. "Black. And a glass of water."

"Same for me," her dad said, still keeping eye contact with Belle.

"Do you have green tea?" Luna asked.

"Sure." Jenn smiled.

"Great."

"Of course." Jenn jotted on her pad. "Have you looked over the menu? Or shall I come back?"

"Can you do oatmeal?" Luna questioned. "Not the kind in the little packets. Too many chemicals and too much sugar. We're vegan, Mom and me, just so you know. Sometimes those are processed with animal stuff."

"Good to know. And yes, we make old-fashioned rolled oats. That work? What would you like in it?"

Luna gave Jenn a smile. "Perfect. Cinnamon. Some walnuts if you have them, and raisins?"

Jenn kept nodding.

"I'll take that, too," Ginger added. "With a side of fruit, if you have some."

More jotting. Jenn glanced at Belle's dad.

"Bacon, two eggs over easy, and wheat toast for me." Grant finally looked at the server. "I'm not vegan." He laughed. "Thanks."

"Got it all. I'll be right back with the your drinks and water." Jenn glanced at Belle and smiled.

"Thanks, Jenn."

"Nice girl," her dad said.

"She's a friend."

"You should have introduced me!"

He's right. But her mind had been elsewhere. "Sorry, Dad. I wasn't thinking."

He tented his hand over the table, staring at his fingers. "Belle, I'm behind you one hundred percent. Whatever decision you make, I'm there. You have my support."

"Mine, too, honey," Ginger said. "Did you know that before I got into real estate, I was a midwife? Well, once a midwife, always a midwife, some people say. If you have questions, I'm happy to share."

She smiled and reached for her hand. Ginger's fingers were as warm as her smile, and Belle curled her own around them. No wonder her dad had fallen in love with her. Belle wasn't sure she'd ever met another person with as kind and sincere a heart as Ginger.

Now Luna? I'm still on the fence.

She'd only spent a few weekends with her dad, Ginger, and her four kids over the past year, so she really didn't know any of them well. From what she had seen, though, Luna came off as distant and a little shallow.

Maybe she's just shy.

"Thanks, Ginger. I didn't know that. But I sure appreciate it. I'll have a ton of questions once I think about it."

"Well, start soon. You're in your eighth month, right?"

Belle nodded. "Yes."

"God, you don't look that pregnant," Luna said. "I mean, you're in great shape."

"I still swim. It's good for my heart and my leg and the baby—according to my doctors."

Her dad shifted in his seat. "I understand you have an OB team here in Tuckaway Bay for when the time comes?"

"Actually, in Nags Head at the hospital. And a cardiology team, but that's just a precaution. They'll patch in the Chicago team. It's all good, Dad. We're ready."

Suddenly, tears spilled over her dad's lower eyelids. "Sorry," he said, swiping them away. "I get emotional sometimes."

"Dad, I'm fine."

"You're going to have a baby. We're going to have a new family member."

"And you're going to be a grandpa."

His eyes went wide, and he grinned even wider. "I can't wait."

Belle's heart melted like butter.

But inside, she felt nervous looking into her dad's eyes. He was a lot more worried and uneasy than he was letting on.

A sudden clattering and banging noise interrupted them. Startled, she jerked, looking toward the front of the restaurant. Zach stood there clanging a wooden spoon on a cookie sheet. "Can I get everyone's attention?"

"What's going on?" Luna asked.

"Not sure." Belle wondered that herself.

"I bet it's the storm," Grant said.

"Sorry to interrupt your meals, everyone," Zach started, "but we have new storm details. Looks like she's making a turn directly toward the Outer Banks north of Cape Hatteras and running up into the eastern mountains. Lots of rain and wind predicted, so we need to get ready."

"How can we help, T-Man?" One of the fishermen called out. "We're ready."

Zach nodded his appreciation. "Thanks. Filling sandbags and boarding up windows. We likely should have jumped on this yesterday, but this storm is acting crazy. But let's see what we can get done."

The four fishermen rose and moved closer to Zach. Belle noticed the younger man of the group quietly step up to Zach and speak. "Not saying we'll need it, but I'm an emergency medical tech, just so you know. I always carry my med bag with me. I brought some other supplies for this trip, too. It's all in the truck. I'll go get that now, then I'll find you."

Zach nodded. "That's awesome, Josh. I hope we just use your strong back and quick hands for nailing boards to walls, but it's great to know we have you—just in case."

Josh smiled slightly, then his expression turned serious as he headed out the door.

Turning back to the crowd in the restaurant, Zach continued. "Sorry to say, folks, that this is an all-hands-on-deck situation. I need help filling sandbags, placing them around the hotel, and boarding up windows. All help is appreciated. If you want to fill sandbags, see Sam. Anyone else who wants to help, come with me." He turned toward the door, then quickly back again. "Oh, and for the duration and for your help, all meals and rooms are on me. Compliments of the resort. Let's get to it."

"Well, that's that. See if she can put my eggs on hold. I'll eat later." Her dad rose from the booth and looked them over. "You three stay here where it's safe. I'll do our part to help."

"We can fill sandbags, Grant." Ginger scooted to the edge of the booth. "Right, Luna?"

Luna tossed her mother what seemed a reluctant nod. "Sure."

"Okay. Fine." Grant looked at Belle. "But you, young lady? Stay here. Find your mother."

"I think she's helping in the kitchen, trying to get ready for Christmas dinner tomorrow. Maybe I can run food and water to everyone."

"That's a plan." He glanced toward the crowd of men gathering around Zach. "Just be careful. See you all later."

———

For all of Luna Jones's seventeen years, she'd never been to the east coast, or North Carolina, and hadn't quite known what to expect. When Grant suggested they fly out to visit Belle for Christmas—because, frankly, he'd been as nervous as a witch's cat in Salem since he'd learned about Belle's pregnancy—she'd envisioned sandy beaches, bright blue sunshiny skies, high wispy clouds, and a crisp breeze.

That's not what she got, however.

Obviously.

Oh, she knew it would be chilly. She was used to damp and chilly. But she hadn't expected a winter monsoon at Christmas.

Growing up in Seattle, she knew all about Pacific northwest living—and all about the rain. While she'd heard of big storms with hurricane-strength winds barreling over the coast in the past—typhoons, they called them—she'd experienced nothing like that in her lifetime. What she had experienced was snow, and rain, and plenty of flooding.

But living in Seattle, that's what one expects—and generally what one gets.

The earthquakes, however, no matter how small, always worried her.

Now, standing under the hotel, behind some dunes that were not doing their job of protecting them from the wind and rain, Luna held a sandbag while her mother shoveled. Looking up at her, she quipped. "Some vacation, huh?"

Her mother paused shoveling for a moment and eyed her. "We all need to help, Luna. This storm could be bad." She dug in the sand again. "Besides, we are grateful to see Belle and happy to have shelter right now. Don't make this difficult, please?"

Luna huffed. She got it. Her mother always looked on the bright side. Her glass was always half-full and filling. And her lemons always turned into lemonade.

Mine? Not so much. "We've done ten of these. Can we stop? I'm wet."

"And so am I."

"A hot shower would feel great right now. Wouldn't it?"

"It will also feel great later."

"I don't see what kind of difference our measly ten bags are going to make with all this water."

Ginger parked her shovel in the sand. "Luna, stop. Be grateful we are here to help. It might only be ten bags, but that could make a difference somewhere, for someone. Here. Let me tie that one up and we'll see how many more we need to do." She glanced around. "Sam! Here's one more."

Sam jogged toward them. "I'll take it. I think we're about to finish up. The wind is getting the best of us."

"Great." Luna said. "I'm heading for the shower."

Her mother grasped her arm, stopping her. "What else can we do, Sam?"

He glanced off, thinking. "Check in with Lia in the Sandcastle kitchen, if you want. I think they are rustling up food. Trying to cook up some things for dinner later, and for a Christmas meal tomorrow, in case we lose power."

"We can do that," Ginger said. "We'll clean up, then go help."

"We're going to lose power?" Luna's voice raised.

Sam met her gaze. "I'd say the chances of that happening are pretty high."

The warning pinch on her arm from her mother's finger stopped her from snapping out something ugly.

"Perfect," she muttered. *Just perfect. Merry Christmas to me.*

THE KITCHEN LIGHTS FLICKERED.

No, no, no, no no... Please don't lose power. The turkeys aren't cooked yet.

Belle glanced overhead at a row of hanging LED utility lights, heaved a long sigh, then pushed a large cookie sheet of day-old bread into the oven and set the timer. Crossing her fingers, she sent up a quick and silent prayer. They had a ton of bread to use up and turkey dressing was on the menu for tomorrow—that is, if the power held out. They had a lot of hungry mouths to feed.

She'd buttered and garlicked both sides of every piece—a trick she'd learned from her grandmother back in Chicago—and arranged them on the sheet, getting as many on as possible, but leaving a bit of space between them so the edges would get crispy.

"Are you feeling okay? You look tired, honey."

Lia moved beside her and pushed a lock of hair from her face, tucking it behind her ear. She looked into her mother's eyes. "It's been a long day so far, Mom. And I have a feeling it's going to get longer. I'm worried about losing power. All this half-cooked food...."

The lights dimmed again. Lia's gaze studied the lamps overhead. "Me, too. I just hope the power holds out long enough for those turkeys to finish roasting."

"And the dressing."

"Oh yes. What else do you have going on over here?"

Belle stepped away and turned. "All the stuff for the dressing is ready once the bread has toasted and cooled. I've chopped celery and onions, cooked the giblets, found some cans of broth in case there's not enough drippings from the turkey." She moved down the kitchen island work-space and opened the walk-in refrigerator door. "I made the deviled eggs already from the eggs you boiled earlier. Peeled potatoes are sitting in water ready to cook. And I made a huge gelatin salad."

Lia peered into the walk-in. "Whew. You've been busy. We might want to pull out those potatoes to get boiling now."

"Okay."

Lia stopped her. "No! I'll get it. That's a big pan. Don't lift that!"

Belle laughed. "Mom. I put it in there."

The look of horror on Lia's face was almost priceless. Her mother pushed past her and retrieved the pan of potatoes and set them on the work island.

"Well, you're pregnant. And you have a heart condition. As long as I am standing and breathing, you are not going to carry this big pan of potatoes or anything else. You hear me?"

Belle let out a lengthy, but silent, exhale. "Yes, ma'am."

Whipping around, Lia shot her a troubled look. "Now, don't ma'am me, Belle Mitchell. I'm worried about you and the baby. Let me do these things."

"Alright. But please stop worrying. Remember what Dr. Speakman said during our last visit to Chicago? My heart is healthy. When they fixed it right after I was born, the surgeons did an excellent job, and with all the swimming, my heart has gotten a really good workout over the years. It's strong. I'm strong, Mom. You know that. Frankly, I practically don't even have a heart condition anymore."

"But childbirth puts strain on every woman's heart, honey. And yours is special." Lia peered into her eyes with misty tears.

"Okay, Mom. All precautions heeded. I'm not carrying heavy stuff." Lia smiled.

Time to change the subject. Belle glanced about at all the prepared food scattered about the workspaces. "Did you do pies, Mom?"

"Pies, yes. Two pumpkin and four pecan. And a huge layer cake, just because we had the ingredients, and I figure kids like cake."

"Good plan. What's next?"

Lia drummed her fingers on the island. "Casseroles? Let's see what veggies we have. And oh, we have greens and such for a big salad."

"Sounds good."

Lia started to make a list.

Belle rubbed her lower back, wishing the ache away that had settled there. She wouldn't say it out loud, but she had been on her feet probably way too long....

"Sweetheart? Have you talked with any of the girls in the last couple of hours?"

"Which set? The old girls, or the young girls?"

Abruptly, Lia turned and gave her a startled look. "And just who are you calling old?"

"Oh, Mom." A bubble of laughter boiled up in Belle's throat and she couldn't help but giggle. "That look on your face is priceless."

"Well, I'm not old. Yet."

"But you'll soon be a grandmother."

"A young and—"

Belle put up a hand and cut her off. "Stop. Young and sexy. I know."

Lia grinned. "So, have you seen the younger girls? I spent a few minutes with Maggie, Alice, and Julia a while ago, but I've not seen the others."

"I've not talked with any of them since breakfast."

"Oh. Well then. You don't know...."

"Know what?"

"About Carol and Ella."

Belle shook her head. "What are you talking about, Mom?"

Suddenly, the door between the kitchen and dining room swung open and slapped closed again. Ginger and Luna moved into the kitchen.

"Hey!" Ginger said. "We finished with the sandbags, took a shower, and are here to help."

"Oh, bless you." Lia whooshed out a breath and gave Ginger a hug.

Belle found that a little humorous. *My mom and my stepmom...? Wow.*

"You're a lifesaver," Lia added.

"We take direction well. Sam said you were cooking." Ginger smiled and looked over at her daughter. "Right, Luna?"

Luna crossed her arms over her chest and smirked at her mom. "Sure. Can't wait to get started."

Belle recognized the sarcasm.

Lia twittered around, looking over the supplies on the table and jerking the walk-in door open again. "Let's see. Could one of you make a salad? There are all kinds of fresh greens and other veggies in the cooler. Make a big one. As big as you can. There are some large bowls in the pantry over there..." She pointed. "And oh, check on salad dressings, too. Or perhaps we can make dressing and just toss it right before we eat."

"I can do that." Luna stepped forward. "I actually do like to cook."

"And she loves salad."

"Use whatever you want. If we lose power, it's all going to go bad, one way or another. Maybe we can eat before that happens."

"Crossing fingers." Ginger moved closer to the potatoes. "How about I get these in some fresh water and start them boiling? I also noticed some dried beans in the pantry. Do you have a pressure cooker? I could make a vegan dish or two real quick with the beans, if that's okay with you."

"Oh, that's right." Belle turned to her mom. "Ginger and Luna are vegan, so we have to make sure we have food for them, too."

Ginger gave her a smile. "You are very sweet, Belle. Luna and I can always find something to eat. Besides, with beans and vegetables, we are good!"

"Great." Lia said, heading toward the pantry shelves. "I'll get the cooker. Make yourself comfortable and cook up a storm." She halted abruptly and turned. "Wait. Not a storm."

Everyone laughed.

Sixteen

For the next hour, they all worked side by side. Belle occasionally chuckled to herself. Ginger and Lia chatted away like they were old friends. She and Luna had a few sidebar conversations. Mostly things from Luna like, "Where can I find..." Or, "Do you know if you have any...."

Whatever. It wasn't that she didn't like Luna. She kind of did. It was more that she hadn't spent enough time with her to get to know her.

Maybe this week after the storm clears.

She had no clue how long her dad intended to stay.

Her new stepsister was a bit of a free spirit, carving her own way in life—much like Ginger. The difference was that Ginger was so sweet and kind and helpful, and Luna generally appeared to react to most things with a laissez-faire, or perhaps an *"are you kidding me?"* attitude.

Leaning against the counter, she exhaled. She was tired, she had to admit. Her feet hurt. And she was a little headachy. Probably the atmospheric pressure from the storm. She rubbed her temples.

Overall, she was cranky and uncomfortable.

Ginger rounded the island and placed an arm over her shoulders. "You okay, honey?"

"She looks a little pale." Her mother joined them.

Great. Two mother hens? She couldn't wait for Alice to get there.

"I'm worried about Belle being on her feet, doing too much." Lia glanced at her ankles. "She looks puffy. Don't you think, Ginger? Maybe you should put your feet up, sweetie, and drink some water. When did you last eat?"

When had she eaten? *Breakfast? Did she even eat then?*

So much going on.

Belle cocked her head and stared. "Mom. I'm fine. There's too much to do and you need my help."

"No. Nada." Ginger stepped forward and grasped Belle's forearm. She pushed a forefinger into the flesh on the back of her hand and looked at her ankles. "Your mom is right. You've got a little edema. Go claim yourself a booth, put your legs up, and Luna will bring you some water and hot tea. Drink them. Okay?"

Belle glanced from her mother to her stepmother and sighed. "I didn't realize how pushy two mothers could be." Then she laughed. "Okay, fine. Following orders."

Ginger held onto her hand. "Are you feeling any pressure? Any discomfort, anywhere?"

Belle shook her head. "No, not really. Just a headache and my lower back aches a little."

"I see." Ginger pursed her lips, nodding. "Okay, go find a seat. We'll bring—"

But she didn't finish her sentence. Something crashed into the side of the hotel, the lights slowly reduced to a dull dim—the storm outside raged against the restaurant. Simultaneously, the door between the dining room and the kitchen burst open.

"You all okay in here?" Zach shouted.

Lia rushed forward. "We're fine! But the power?"

"We may lose it any second, but we still should be okay in here. If that happens, the generator should kick in, but it will only power a few lights, the ovens, and the walk-in. Go get those battery powered lights in the pantry in case and that large portable charging station." Zach spoke fast and with immediacy.

Belle took a breath and pressed her lower back into the edge of the kitchen island. *There, that feels better.* Suddenly, her headache felt worse, though.

"I've already done that," Lia told him. "All those things are over there on the counter."

"Great."

"Are we in danger, Zach?"

Belle noticed the look he gave her mom. "I'm asking everyone to shelter in place in the restaurant. I don't want people on the upper floors. They will all be coming down soon."

"Oh! Do we need to go get things?"

Zach shook his head. "Stay here. I had housekeeping bring blankets and pillows down for us, then I told them to go home to their families. Some opted to stay here, but most left. We don't need to go back up. I'll find a corner for us to hunker down."

The kitchen door waved open again and Sam sprinted in. "Zach! There you are. I have a broken window in my suite. Damn wooden beach chair got tossed up onto the deck and hit the window like it was nothing. This wind is something else."

He rotated toward Sam. "Shit. Let's get something to board it up, stop some of the rain."

"Where's Grant?" Ginger moved forward.

"Finishing up outside with the other men. He'll be in soon."

Luna stepped closer to her mother. "Should we go upstairs and get our things?" She looked at Zach. Belle could tell she was frightened.

"Quickly." Zach said. "Get blankets, pillows, whatever you think you will need. Be back here in five."

"Will do." Ginger nodded and tugged at Luna's hand. "Let's go."

They hurried off toward the dining room.

Belle listened to the exchange, taking in the urgency in Zach's voice, the worried look on her mother's face, and wondered about her dad. He needed to get inside.

Suddenly, she felt something warm and wet between her legs. Glancing down, she saw a small puddle on the floor at her feet. It definitely wasn't rainwater.

"Mom?"

Lia turned and faced her. "It's okay, Belle. I know you're frightened. Zach will keep us safe."

"It's not that."

Zach took a step. "I checked the weather, sweetheart. This should move out of here by morning. We just need to get through the night."

A pain rolled across Belle's lower back then and coiled toward her pelvis. She bent forward with a growly moan. *Get through the night hell!*

"Belle!"

Her mother was instantly at her side. "What's going on?"

The pain rolled on, then subsided. Belle straightened, blew out a shaky breath, and looked directly into her mother's eyes. "My water just broke."

"Oh, shit." Zach didn't mince words.

"Oh, my baby!" Lia hugged her and held her close.

Almost too close.

"We need to find a place for her to lie down, Zach. A cot or something. A rollaway. Don't we have some in storage?"

"Yes."

"Then get one. Now!"

Belle looked back and forth between the two. "No! I am not having my baby in this kitchen, on a dirty rollaway cot that's been in storage since 1949! Get me to the hospital. Now!"

Zach took her hands. "Let's just find a place for you to lie down, get you comfortable, and I'll call 9-1-1 for an ambulance."

"Great." She nodded. "Yes. Do that." She jerked toward her mother. "And find dad!"

Lia pulled her phone from her apron pocket and started texting. Belle noticed her shaking fingers.

"Sorry. It's okay, Mom. I didn't mean to yell." She locked eyes with her mother and then sucked in a breath. Another uneasy, queasy, take-her-breath away pain was starting again.... "Ooooh. Oh! My. God. Aren't these...?"

"Coming too fast? Yes. Sweetheart, you need to lie down."

"Oh, shit... Where? On the floor?"

"Get her a chair. Here!" Zach rolled the kitchen office chair over and set the brake. "Here you go, sweetheart."

Belle eased herself into the soft leather chair.

The kitchen door crashed open and a few more people burst into the room.

"Belle!"

Her vision was blurry, but she knew that was her dad's voice. "Daddy!"

Lia burst into tears. "Oh, Grant."

"I'm here, sweetheart. Ginger's coming, too." He looked at Lia. "She's a midwife. Did you know?"

"No. Oh, thank God."

Ginger and Luna rushed in. "How close are your contractions?" Ginger asked.

"Too. Close."

"I was afraid of that. How long had your back been hurting earlier?"

"A couple of hours. Oh... God."

Another pain.

Grant pulled out his phone. "I'm calling Ned."

"Good. Get him on the phone, Grant." Lia said.

Belle suddenly had a moment of clarity. "And call Dr. Christman at OBX hospital. Mom, go upstairs and get my birth plan. It's on my nightstand. A pink notebook. All the important stuff is in there."

"That's good," Ginger said. "We'll need that."

"But I'm staying here. Zach, get it," Lia barked.

He huffed out a nervous breath. "Sure. Nightstand. Pink notebook."

He was gone in seconds.

Ginger shouted. "Clear off this kitchen island. STAT! I need towels —clean, white towels, soft ones. Let's disinfect this island as much as we can. And blankets. Find blankets and pillows."

People started scurrying.

"What can I do, Mom?" Luna asked Ginger, then met Belle's gaze. "I know you're scared. I'll stay with you, okay? I'm actually training to be a midwife, too."

For some crazy reason, Belle wanted to cry. "Hold my hand, please?"

"Of course. You're my sister."

Belle burst into tears. "Thank you," she whispered. She caught Luna's misty-eyed gaze. "Aunt Luna."

Her stepsister smiled.

"I need a few more things," Ginger said, basically to anyone within earshot. "Candles, soft music. Anyone have an old boom box? CDs? Incense? And we need to lower these lights if we can."

Then she directed Lia. "I also need gloves. Is she allergic to latex?"

"Well, apparently, because she didn't use a condom...."

"Lia! Is she...?"

"No!"

"Ginger, I can't have... the baby... here."

Ginger's voice softened. "Sweetheart, this baby is coming, whether it's here, or in a car heading to the hospital, or in an ambulance... And to be totally honest, you want to be here rather than out stuck in this storm."

Zach burst in. "Got the pink notebook!" He proudly laid it in Lia's hands, like he'd accomplished something major. Belle had to smile at that.

"Also called 9-1-1. Lines are down in places and the power is out at the hospital. Their generator can only handle so much. They will send an ambulance ASAP but they are moving critical patients to another facility. We might be on our own for a while."

"How long?" Lia prodded.

Zach just stared at her.

"Zach?"

"Several hours."

"Nooooo!"

Zach redirected his attention. "Ginger, I brought Josh. He can help."

Belle looked at the young man. *Oh no.* Not "hot guy". Not "hot guy" looking at her... whatever. "No."

"I'm an EMT," Josh said to Ginger. "I've delivered several babies. I can help."

"Good. Watch her vitals. Luna, keep her calm and quiet. I'll monitor the labor and birth. Lia, you are the official birth coach and in charge of the pink notebook. Got it?"

Lia eagerly nodded and said shakily. "I'll also be the go-between with Ned Speakman, Belle's heart doctor." She turned to Grant. "Give me your phone when you get him on the line."

Belle watched her mother's facial expression and knew she was scared to death.

Ginger looked intensely at Belle. "New plan, honey. We're your team. Josh, Luna, your mom, and me. Consider me your doctor. You'll have to trust us. Okay?"

No, no, no... Not this way!

"Belle?"

"I can't do this."

Ginger moved in closer, taking both Belle's hands in hers. "You can, Belle. Believe me. You can do this. I'm not promising it's going to be easy, but when it's all said and done, you are going to have a beautiful baby."

Another pain rolled around her back to her lower pelvis. Belle clutched Ginger's hands. "Oohhh. No. I'm going to be a terrible mother! I can't!"

Ginger squeezed her hands again. "You can, Belle. You're going to be a wonderful mother. "Now, we need to get to work." She handed Belle's hands off to Luna.

"It's okay," Luna whispered, making eye contact. "I've got you."

"Okay." The word burst from her mouth on a breath.

"Great." Ginger nodded. "Josh, help me get her up on the table. The rest of you clear out. You too, Grant and Zach."

"No, I need to be here. I'm her dad."

Zach stepped up. "And I'm the stepdad."

Ginger forced out a quick breath. "While I appreciate your wanting to be here, you can't. In a normal world, that might be fine if Belle was on board with it," Ginger said. "But this is not a normal world, and we want Belle to be comfortable, and I can't have you men in my way. If we need you, I know you'll be right outside that door. Now, go."

"Alright." Zach tossed a smile at Belle. "Later, sweetie."

Grant hesitated. "But...."

"Zach. Get him out. Now."

Her dad left.

Zach left.

Belle glanced about at the onlookers.

This was her team, indeed. Her mom, stepmom, stepsister, and a hot EMT named Josh.

Carol will be jealous.

Suddenly, the lights went out, and the room fell into dark silence. The whirl of the walk-in refrigerator motor gradually stopped. All Belle could hear was her own heartbeat.

After a few seconds, her mother whispered, "Wait for it."

Please work, generator.

The ache that crept along her back then and settled in her lower tummy had her clutching her stomach, screwing up her face, and breaking the strange silence with a snarly cry.

"Shiiiiit," she hissed.

A moment later, the lights flickered back on, much dimmer than before, and the refrigerator hummed.

"Come on, Belle," Ginger said softly. "Let's have a baby."

A WAVE OF CRUSHING AGONY RIPPED ACROSS HER LOWER back, rolled over her abdomen, and increased the pressure in her pelvis. It always started as a dull ache that tightened and pulled until she was curled into a sitting position on the table. Her mother sat behind her on the table too, mostly just holding her upright.

"I need to push!"

"Not yet, sweetheart. Hold on." Ginger examined her. "Almost."

I can't do this. I can't do this. I can't do this!

"I'm. Done."

The two words barely escaped her lips.

The screaming in her brain differed from the words bursting from her mouth—but the sentiment was the same. She was done. Couldn't go any further. *I can't do this.* Her head hurt. Her body was drained of any will or strength she had ever possessed. She had very little energy, even to speak, let alone push a baby out of her hoo-ha.

"No, Belle. Not yet." Her mother whispered in her ear. "You can do this."

A calm, male voice came from her left. "You've got this, Belle. We're going to do this together. Okay?" Josh sat beside her, cooing softly in her ear, trying to keep her calm. There was a blood pressure cuff on her arm and periodically, he'd check it. He'd been there the entire time—but she had no concept of time right now.

Am I fading in and out of consciousness?

"How. Long."

"Let's breathe evenly, okay?" he said. "To keep your blood pressure down, your pulse steady."

Someone patted her shoulders behind her. "Listen to Josh, honey. He's really good at what he does."

"Mom?"

"Yes. I'm right here. Not going anywhere."

"Good."

Josh breathed in and out slowly, coaxing her to do the same between contractions. Her eyes closed, and she listened for his soft, calming voice. Hung on to it, actually. Soothing.

"Luna?" She lifted her right hand. She'd been there earlier. "Where?"

"She stepped out to find a bathroom."

"Oh."

Josh squeezed her hand. "I'm here. Your mom is here. Ginger too."

"How much...longer...?"

"We're close, Belle. I know it's been hell on you, but I'm glad labor went fast. Less stress on you and the baby. With the next contraction, we are going to push. Okay?" Ginger's voice came from somewhere near her legs.

We? We? What is this we shit? I'm the only one pushing!

"Josh, watch her pressure and pulse. Lia, help her push. Luna, glad you are back. It's go time."

The pelvic pain rolled and then burst upon her, the pressure exploding against her cervix. The intensity was strong, too much, and she felt herself falling...fading....

"Belle! Push!"

"Can't." She shook herself into awareness.

"Now, honey."

Luna clutched her hand. "We got this, sister."

"You're doing great, Belle," Josh said. "Eyes open. Keep breathing. There."

The pain deepened. She mustered up one loud long explosion of words. "IfIeverseethatstupidChadwhatshisnameagainIwillfuck-ingkillhim!"

The contraction ceased and the pain gradually subsided. Belle lay back against her mother's chest, breathing heavily, sweating. "I... Can't."

"You can, Belle. You're strong," her mother whispered. "All you need to do is concentrate on the joy you are going to feel when it's all over."

"Like swimming...in competition."

"That's right. Just picture the other side of the pool in your head. Do whatever you need to do to get there, sweetheart. You can do this."

Belle huffed out a breath. "Touch the other side. Be first. Win the race," she said slowly.

"You are a winner already, honey. At the end of this, you'll have a beautiful child."

She smiled. "Yes."

"One more time. Get ready," Ginger said. "This is it. This is the one."

"Oooohhhh.... Shit!" The contraction curled and pulled and tight-ened across her pelvis. She rolled herself into a comma shape, facing Ginger. Her mother supporting her, Luna and Josh holding her hands.

"Push!"

She pushed with everything in her, visualizing the side of the pool. Picturing her baby's face. "Grrrrrr... Oooh... God, please. Get this baby out now! Ahhhhh!"

In one fell swoop, suddenly, it was over.

"She's here!" Ginger exclaimed. "Luna, get those soft towels."

A squeaky baby cry sounded from between her legs.

"She?" Belle tried to sit up further. "My baby? It's a girl? Is she okay?"

A full-blown cry was her answer.

"She's small but perfect."

The baby's cries continued, louder now.

"And feisty!" Ginger added.

"It's a girl?" Lia repeated.

Another pain hit Belle. She clutched both Josh and Luna's hands until the pain moved through—but this one wasn't as bad.

Ginger stood, smiling, tears in her eyes, and rounded the island. She handed the bundle in her arms to Belle. "Here is your beautiful girl, Belle."

She couldn't help but burst into tears, looking down into her sweet baby's face. Joy for seeing her for the first time, and relief that it was all over.

"Oh, Mom," she whispered.

"She's beautiful." Lia pulled the towel back from the baby's cheek a little. A tear from her mother's eyes fell on the baby's forehead. She softly rubbed it into her skin. "What's her name?"

Belle had thought about names, but nothing she'd landed on had seemed right—until this moment. She met her mother's gaze. "Grace. Her name is Grace."

Lia smiled.

Ginger glanced at her phone. "That was Grant. The ambulance is here. Let's get both of you checked out at the hospital."

"Oh, that's good... But the storm?"

"Honey, the wind and rain subsided a couple of hours ago. The storm is over."

Seventeen

Christmas Morning

Since she'd had no concept of time for hours, and the curtains in her hospital room were drawn tight, Belle wasn't sure what time of day, or night, it was.

She'd slept, apparently, and for quite a while.

The flurry of activity to get her and baby Grace to the hospital by ambulance, then both of them getting checked over by Dr. Christman, her OB/GYN team, the pediatrician, and calls to Dr. Speakman and her cardiovascular team, was almost more tiring than labor.

That was a lie. Nothing was more tiring than labor!

She'd been able to snuggle with little Grace on the way, and her heart had never been so full, or felt so alive. Once they'd arrived at the hospital, they'd swept her one way, the baby another.

Before long, all the experts had concluded that she and baby Grace were healthy.

She'd talked with Dr. Speakman, who had reviewed all her vitals and spoke with Ginger. He was pleased.

Dr. Christman had praised Ginger for the delivery and Josh for the assist.

They'd even teased that if all went well over the next hours, she and baby Grace could possibly be released in time for Christmas dinner.

By the time all that was through, though, she'd been exhausted. The nurse recommended she let the baby sleep in the nursery for a while, instead of in her room, so Belle could get some rest.

Her mother insisted. She agreed. And now, here she was, sometime later, waking up.

Glancing about, a sliver of light poked through the crack in the nearly closed door. She was hooked up to a few monitors, which were blinking and beeping beside her. Shifting positions in the bed, she searched for the button to raise her upper body, found it, then moved into a semi-sitting position.

There. That didn't hurt too much.

Great.

Did I just have a baby? She chuckled to herself.

Someone sat in a chair in the darkened corner of the room, close to the foot of her bed. Sleeping, perhaps?

"Mom?"

The person moved and slowly eased up. "Hey. You're awake."

Not mom. A man's voice. "Oh. Who...?"

Josh crossed the sliver of light from the door and approached her bed. "Hi."

"Hi?" *Why is he here?*

"Want me to open the curtains a little?"

"Please. It's dark."

"Just a bit. The sun is bright today." He pulled back the heavy hospital curtains and a larger stream of light flooded the room. "You slept for several hours."

"Grace? Is she okay?"

He took a step closer. "Nurse says she's doing fine."

Good. Her little baby. "Wow, it is bright."

"Too much?"

She shook her head. "No. Feels good. The storm is really over?"

"Yes." He moved closer to the bed. "We survived." The smile on his face warmed Belle's heart a little. Brief remembrances of him holding her hand through the labor, talking softly into her ear, flitted by.

"I thought I'd stay a while until you woke up."

Belle sighed. "That was nice of you, Josh. Thank you. And thanks for keeping me sane through all that, um…ugliness. Apologies for the slew of nasty words I let fly."

He laughed, and that made her smile, too. "You were a model patient. I've seen worse."

"I doubt that." She studied him as he glanced about the room.

"Well, you were."

An uneasy pause settled over the room.

"Thanks for being there, Josh. It was comforting knowing a medical professional was in the room. Not that I don't trust Ginger but having you there was… reassuring, like I said."

His gaze drifted back to meet hers and held for several seconds. "I'm glad I could help."

Belle remembered something then. "Did you ride with me in the ambulance, too? Everything was sort of fuzzy."

With a nod, he said, "I did."

"Well, thanks for that, too."

"You're welcome." He paused this time, keeping eye contact. "By the way, Grace is the sweetest thing. I stepped over to the nursery earlier, while your mom was here with you."

"Mom? Where is she?"

He glanced at the door. "She slept here for a while. She was exhausted, too. I told her I'd stay while she got something to eat. She's in the cafeteria with the rest of your crew."

"My crew? Oh, goodness… All of them?"

Josh laughed. "They are quite the handful. The nurses ordered them off the floor because they were noisily gathering at your door, and then at the nursery windows. You know they are an enthusiastic bunch."

"That's my crew, for sure."

"Your mom should be here soon."

"And they let you stay?"

He gave her a cockeyed grin. "I flashed 'em my medical creds."

"Ha! That's funny, Josh."

Moving closer, he carefully laid his hand over hers, softly caressing her fingers. "I wanted to stay. I hope you don't mind."

He stared into her eyes for a moment. Belle felt his sincerity. "I'm glad you stayed," she mumbled.

The door pushed inward.

"Belle! You're awake. Oh, sweetheart."

Josh slipped his hand away and stepped back from the bed, allowing Lia to move in closer. His gaze lingered with Belle's though, momentarily. Finally, he moved toward the door.

"Mom! I had a baby!"

Laughing, Lia bent over the bed to hug her. "That you did."

Josh glanced over his shoulder as he exited. She gave him a little finger wave. He nodded, tossed up one hand, and smiled.

Then he was gone.

"Do you want to see baby Grace? Oh, my God, sweetheart. She is the most perfect little human. I am already infatuated with this child. Oh, and I was just talking with the nurse..." Lia bubbled over with excitement as she sat on the corner of Belle's bed. "They are planning to bring her in soon. The breastfeeding coach will be here shortly too, to go over some things. According to the pink notebook, you want to breast-feed, right? So that is happening. And of course, everyone is here wanting to see you and Grace but those nurses...."

"I heard."

"Well, they said we could have a few people at a time in your room, so Maggie and I made a plan. Shifts for visitors. As long as you don't get tired out. So, the first shift is your dad—who is just simply beside himself with joy—and Ginger and Luna... And then Zach—who, by the way, cried when I told him you named the baby Grace."

"Oh, Mom. He didn't."

"He did. You really touched his heartstrings."

"It just felt right."

Lia grinned wide. "You okay with visitors after baby Grace is here for a while?"

"Sure."

"Good. Then after Zach will come Maggie and Julia."

"Alright."

"Then Carol and Hannah."

"What about Alice and Ella?"

Lia froze and pursed her lips. "Oh, that's right. You don't know about Ella."

"Mom?"

"Ella was sort of AWOL for a while... But George found her and she's at Alice's house right now. Sleeping. Alice is over there too. I guess they had a scary night."

"Oh, goodness."

Lia patted her forearm. "We'll probably see them all later. It's quite a story. Now...."

A knock sounded at the door and a nurse poked her head inside. "Anyone ready to see their little Christmas miracle?"

"Oh, my." Belle sighed and met her mother's gaze. "Grace was born on Christmas? I didn't realize."

"Yes, honey. We have a little Christmas package here for you."

The nurse pushed the bassinet inside and rolled it next to Belle's bed. There, in the small transparent cubicle, lay her precious sleeping bundle, wearing a red Santa hat and a red, green, and white striped onesie.

"Omigoodness," she breathed. "So stinking cute."

In the next instant, the room filled with people. Her dad, who was overcome with emotion, burst into tears when he saw her. Luna and Ginger consoled him. Then Zach came, kissing her on the forehead, a wild grin on his face. Maggie, Julia, Sam, and Hannah followed.

Then Josh. They made eye contact from across the room. He gently smiled.

Everyone crowded around the bed, oohing and aahing, and noisily chattering away.

The nurse took a step back, shook her head and grinned broadly, then walked out of the room and closed the door.

"LIA, SLOW DOWN. YOU'RE GOING TO COLLAPSE IF YOU don't."

"That's rich, coming from you, Mr. Allen. You haven't stopped checking on damages and moving debris and taking down boards since we got back from the hospital!"

Zach grinned. "Touché. You're right. But things need to be done. We have guests."

"Oh, pooh. The staff will work on that as soon as they get back here. But today is Christmas, and we have a new baby coming home in a few hours."

"Which is why you need to rest."

"Me? I'm fine," Lia argued. "Belle is the one who will need rest. My goodness, that girl gave it all she had during labor. And now, the baby is going to require attention, too. Her hands are going to be full, and she'll need my help."

"Which is precisely why you should slow down and conserve a bit of that energy."

Lia cocked her head to the side, thinking. "I hate it when you're right."

Leaning in, he kissed her nose.

She smiled up at him. "I need to get this food ready, though. We cooked up nearly everything we had, and we have hungry people who want to eat it. The people here last night barely made a dent in what we made.

"Now, since you have so much energy, how about helping me rearrange the tables in the dining area so we can have one big, long festive table for all of us to sit at and eat?"

"I'll get Sam and Grant to help me with that. You mind the kitchen, woman."

Lia stuck out her tongue and turned away.

Zach swatted her on her rear.

"Anyone need help around here?"

Lia and Zach turned as Sam and Julia joined them.

"We figure you two are likely swamped," Sam said.

"As a matter of fact…" Zach began. "We need to move some tables and chairs. Up for it?"

"Definitely."

Julia approached Lia. "I'm sure you need help with the food, right?"

"Oh, bless you." Lia leaned in and whispered to her. "I don't want to admit it to Zach, but I'm dead on my feet. Yes, I can use the help. Please!"

Julia gave her a hug. "I swear, baby Grace is the cutest baby ever, Grammy. Is that what she's going to call you? Grammy?"

With a sigh, Lia said, "I suppose she'll call me whatever she wants. I'm already wrapped around her little finger."

"Well, let's get this Christmas meal together so little Grace and her mom can have the perfect Christmas homecoming." Julia hooked her arm in Lia's.

Abruptly, the restaurant door banged open again.

"We're here! What can we do?" Maggie shouted.

Carol and Hannah followed her inside.

"Me too." Grant poked his head in the door. "Ginger and Luna are on their way. They took quick power naps. But we figure there are things to be done."

"Got that right, Grant!" Zach moved toward him.

Behind them, entered the three fishermen and Josh.

"We in da house too, T-Man!" Chuckers called out. "Tomorrow, we fish. Today, we clean up and eat!"

"Alright! Yeah!" Monk and Otter shouted.

Josh shook his head at his father and friends.

"Okay, before we all get busy, I have one question."

Everyone turned toward Lia.

"What's that, honey?" Zach gave her his full attention.

"Why the heck do your hockey friends call you T-Man?"

At that, Josh paled a little and glanced at his buddies.

Chuckers guffawed. "That's short for Turtle-Man, Lia." He laughed again. "Zach here was the slowest damn skater on the team. In fact, one year we embroidered a turtle on his jersey."

"But I had a mean slap shot, though," Zach said. "You gotta admit that."

"That you did, brother."

Zach looked at her and shrugged. "What can I say? I'm slow but methodical, and in the end, I get the job done."

This time, Lia laughed as loud as the hockey players. Throwing her arms around his neck, she whispered, "I will definitely not argue with that technique, T-Man."

Zach grinned and kissed her cheek.

Lia stepped back, smiling, and gazed out into the dining room at all their friends, grateful for each and every crazy one of them. Hands on hips, she said, "Well then. It's time to get busy. We have a baby coming home for Christmas."

THE CHATTER AROUND THE TABLE WAS ALMOST DEAFENING. Belle sat in the middle of the string of chairs on one side and glanced from one end of the table to the other. Hot and cold food dishes covered every available inch of table space, with the desserts placed on the counter behind them. Zach stood at one end carving a turkey and her dad at the other, slicing a ham. Sam had just said a quick blessing over the food.

Belle sighed. Home. Family. Friends.

What more could a girl ask for?

Love?

Time for that down the road. Today, she was totally, incredibly, and adorably infatuated with her baby Grace. Not to mention, absolutely blessed with her extended family and friends.

That's all the love she needed.

The conversation around the table continued. Flatware clanked against bowls and plates.

"Maggie," Julia asked. "I never heard you say. Did you and the kids have your Christmas Eve call with Max? How's Australia?"

Carol and her mother exchanged a glance—like they were passing a secret between the two of them. Belle listened with interest.

"Well," Maggie began. "Max was sort of busy and we...well, seems we got our times mixed up."

"Actually," Carol said, "He had something else going on and it appeared he was quite busy. But it's okay. We will talk to him soon." She turned to her mother. "Right, Mom?"

Maggie looked into her lap. "Yes, that's right. Very soon." She sidled her gaze to her daughter then. "Carol did get a quick chat with him later, but Jason and Chloe didn't. We'll try him tomorrow."

Julia eyed Maggie. "Oh. I see. How long did you say he's staying in Australia?"

Carol blurted out. "Probably indefinitely. And we're okay with it, aren't we Mom?" Carol leaned closer to her mother and laid her head on her shoulder.

Maggie stroked her cheek and hair. "Perfectly okay with it," she whispered.

Lia and Julia and Alice stared at Maggie and Carol.

Carol fingered a pretty gold necklace around her neck.

"That's a beautiful locket," Belle said. "So pretty."

Sitting up, Carol smiled. "It's gold. Thanks. It was a gift." She looked at Maggie. "From my mom."

Maggie smiled and brushed away a tear.

Lia and Julia and Alice still stared at the mother-daughter duo.

Belle thought it almost comical.

Maggie turned to her left then and changed the subject. "So, Ella, I need to hear all about this adventure you had during the storm. What the heck happened?"

Ella and Alice exchanged looks, but said nothing.

"Oh," Maggie said. "But if it's not something you want to talk about..." She glanced at Julia and then Lia. "Maybe I should have kept my big mouth shut!"

"It's okay." That came from George, who was sitting beside Ella, just to Belle's right. "Let's say we all had a trying afternoon, but things improved later in the day."

Ella heaved out a sigh. "I think most of you know that Mom and I had a fight. I got mad. And in a huff, I took the car and left. I planned to go to the cabin and stay the weekend with Dad, but the weather and the car had other ideas. My cell phone died, and I ran out of gas, but thankfully, I made it to an overpass and sheltered there from the storm."

"Of course, I was frantic," Alice interjected. "When George finally retrieved his voice mails, and realized Ella had set out for the mountains, he headed east along the route he knew Ella would take."

"Eventually, he spotted our car under the overpass."

"I called Alice ASAP and she met me at our house. We rode out the storm there. Fortunately, we didn't lose power on the sound side."

Carol leaned forward. "Oh my God, Ella. I bet you were so scared in that car alone."

Ella's expression grew serious. "It was not my most favorite night ever!" She smiled at Carol. "And by the way, I'm sorry for those things I said the other day."

Carol waved her off. "Forgotten." Then, pausing for a few seconds, she added. "Same. I'm sorry."

The table fell silent for a moment.

Finally, Hannah tossed the girls a half-grin and said, "Well, that was good for the soul. Cleansing. I hope."

Carol rolled her eyes.

Ella laughed.

Belle shook her head.

Luna interjected. "I think I'm missing something."

All the younger group of women laughed. Belle nudged Luna, who was sitting beside her. "I'll fill you in later. We need to get you up to speed."

"Apparently!"

Zach dinged a table knife on his glass then. "Before we dig in too deep with food and conversation, I'd just like to say a couple of things, if you don't mind."

The entire group grew silent, except for a few baby coos coming from the impromptu bassinet Zach and Grant made that afternoon from an old dresser drawer and some soft pillows.

He cleared his throat. "To Belle, my beautiful and brave stepdaughter, who is going to be an awesome mother. We are so proud of you, each and every one of us. We all love you so much.

"And to baby Grace, who I hope will live up to all the crazy shenanigans experienced by my own Aunt Grace.

"To my beautiful wife and sexy grandma, Lia. I wish you years of love, happiness, and many joyful Christmases to come. I can't wait to spend them all right here with our growing family.

"And to our friends—we are blessed. Truly blessed to have you in our lives. Every single one of you is unique and we love you for it. Your help and support the past couple of days goes unsurpassed, and you have our eternal thanks. While we literally had a stormy Christmas, in so many ways, we got through it because we have each other."

Zach paused momentarily, sniffling a little, and eyed Lia. "And now, the words coming out of my mouth next are going to be a total surprise to my wife—but I'm going to put a stake in the ground and say them, right here and right now."

He paused dramatically. "Let's gather here again next year. And the year after that. Let's make this a tradition!"

Cheers went up across the table.

Lia stood. "Zach Allen, I hope you know I am going to hold you to that—but can we ditch the storm?"

"And the drama?" Hannah added.

Maggie laughed. "I make no guarantees."

Laughter bubbled up and the Christmas chaos continued.

Once everyone had pushed back from the table, Lia insisted on a photo. "Who has a camera with a delay function so we can all get into the picture? I want to send it to Wren and Willow—and of course, all of us, too."

"Great idea," Julia said.

"Agreed!" Maggie added.

"I can do that," George said. "Just let me get it set up."

Lia gathered the group in front of the table. After a few moments of propping the phone and selecting the proper settings, he said, "Alright. Five seconds. Everyone ready?"

Belle watched him dash off to settle in next to Alice on her left.

While she held baby Grace, standing in the center of the group, she smiled and waited for the flash.

Suddenly, an overwhelming sense of contentment washed over her. She was home. These were her people.

And as much as she'd resented the fact that the mystery Chad had abandoned her, she was suddenly grateful. Everyone standing around her loved her, her child, and each other.

That's all she needed.

"Cheese!"

The camera flashed.

George rushed to his phone, fiddled with a few settings, then sent the picture to Alice, who then sent it to the girls' group.

"Oh my," Lia whispered after a minute. "We are a motley crew, aren't we? Should we take another?"

But the group had scattered. The moment lost.

She showed the picture to Belle.

It wasn't a picture-perfect picture.

George was blurry. Carol was looking at her mom. Chloe and Jason were shoving each other. Zach was kissing Lia's cheek, while Lia stared down at the baby.

Sam grinned widely, his arms wrapped around both Julia and Hannah's shoulders. Belle had to laugh—he was the only one looking at the camera. Alice stared blankly at Ella, who was looking over at her dad. Grant and Ginger and Luna stood behind her, Luna's fingers touching Grace's little head. The fishermen were rough housing, as usual—except for Josh.

Josh stood a few feet away, looking at her. She stared down at baby Grace.

Her Christmas miracle.

The picture *was* perfect.

Just perfect.

Epilogue

Belle woke several hours later, her phone pinging a message.

Groggily, she scooted up in her bed and grasped her phone, trying to be quiet so she wouldn't wake Grace. She didn't turn on a light for that reason, either.

Who in the world would text at this hour?

Everyone at the inn had turned in early because most guests were checking out in the morning. And frankly, the storm had left everyone exhausted.

Maggie and her kids were leaving early. The fishermen were heading out to sea on a charter boat before sunrise, then heading home in a couple of days.

Sam and Julia and Hannah were going back to Sam's place on the sound—but Sam had promised to be back to help with cleanup. Her dad and Ginger and Luna decided to hang around for a few more days, and she was glad about that.

So who was texting?

She pushed the notification and noticed the number was not one she knew or had saved to her contacts. She didn't like to open things from people she didn't know—but for some reason, she felt compelled to read it.

She opened the message. The text held only a video. She tapped to get it started.

The file showed Wren and Willow standing on a wooden deck, a monstrous snow-capped mountain behind them, blue skies above. They were dressed in winter gear, like they'd been out skiing. Willow balanced a chubby baby in a snowsuit on her hip.

Both women looked healthy and happy.

Wren started talking. "Belle, honey, we are so proud of you! Your mom sent us the group picture earlier. While I know we've been AWOL for so long, we hope to remedy that situation soon."

Willow piped up. "Yes! And we can't wait to meet baby Grace! She is so precious. I need to introduce her to Charlotte here." She smiled down at the chubby baby in her arms. "Please tell your mom and the others that we are fine. That we miss them. We hope to see you next Christmas, if not before."

"Yes," Wren added. "Still figuring some things out."

"But we love you, honey. Congrats! Bye!"

They waved.

The video stopped.

She swiped it away.

After a minute, she looked again at the message. It was sent only to her, not her mother and the other girlfriends.

Why?

Did they want her to share the video with them?

Her fingers flew over the small keyboard, typing a quick reply.

Belle: *Thank you! Should I share this with Mom?*

She waited. No response.

Thank You!

I hope you enjoyed reading The Christmas Storm. If so, please help others find this book by leaving a review at your favorite bookstore, or on my website at:

https://maddiejamesbooks.com/products/the-christmas-storm

Have you read these Tuckaway Books?

Beach Therapy
The Space in Between

Aunt Grace's Holiday Snickerdoodle Cookies

Ingredients

Topping

1 ½ teaspoons cinnamon

1 teaspoon cardamon

3 tablespoons fancy sugar—red and green

Cookies

1 cup unsalted butter, room temperature

1¼ cups granulated sugar

1 large egg + 1 large egg yolk

2 teaspoons cream of tartar

1 teaspoon baking soda

1 teaspoon vanilla extract

½ teaspoon sea salt

2¾ cups all-purpose flour

Directions

- Preheat the oven to 375°F.
- Prepare cookie sheets, lightly greased or parchment paper.

- Make topping. Mix the fancy sugar, cinnamon, and cardamon in a flat bowl.
- Cream the butter and the remaining 1¼ cups sugar until light and fluffy.
- Add the egg and yolk and beat until creamy.
- Add the cream of tartar, baking soda, vanilla, and salt. Mix.
- Gradually add the flour and mix until just combined. DO NOT OVERMIX!
- Scoop about 2 T. of dough and roll into a ball. Make sure all are the same size.
- Roll the dough balls in the cinnamon sugar.
- Place on cookie sheets about 2 inches apart.
- Bake 8 to 9 minutes. If you like them chewy, remove after 8 minutes. If you like them crisp, add another minute or so. Cool for 10 minutes on the sheet then remove.

A Peek into Maggie's Future

Maggie jerked away from Max and his snarly, cocky attitude. She couldn't look at him any longer.

"Are you insane, Max? What exactly are you suggesting?"

"I think you get it, Mags. Look. We can make this work, and the kids will never have to know. You stay here in the states, I'll come home now and again, and Lily and I and the baby will live in Brisbane."

Maggie threw up her hands and stomped off. Gazing out her bedroom window, she said, "You can't have your cake and eat it too."

"I can't?" He snickered. "I seemed to have managed that so far."

She looked at him. He was right. And she'd let him, dammit. "No, not this time. Because I won't let that happen."

"Right."

"You are a fucking asshole, Max."

He laughed. "You're right. I am." His grin fell into a frown. "Don't fight this. We can make it work, and no one will know. The beauty of it all is that Lily is half-way around the world."

"And no one *there* has to know, either."

He ambled closer, that stupid cock-ass grin on his face. "Look Mags. You have it good here. I'll send the money and pay the bills like always. Nothing has to change. You all stay in the house, the kids go to their private schools, and you keep the fringe benefits of being my wife. Besides, you don't want to mess this up for the kids. I know you will do anything for those kids. And I mean, anything."

He paused, looking her over.

She felt like a piece of meat at the butcher shop.

"Carol has college coming up real soon. How could you pay for that without me?"

Bastard.

"Scholarships? Student loans? How do you think regular people pay for things like that? I'll find a way."

"I don't think so. You don't want to strap Carol with student loan debt."

No, she didn't. But she also didn't want to chain herself to Max for the rest of her life. Or Carol. Mostly, she wanted to separate the kids from depending on him too much because, frankly, with him having another family in Australia, how long could that last? At some point, she was going to have to disappoint them and tell the kids the truth.

Wait. Was that the thing she could hold over his head?

"On one condition, Max."

"What's that?"

"I'll go along with this two-family charade if, and only if, you go in there right now and tell the kids the truth. That you cheated on me, and often, and that you have another family in Brisbane. That's my condition."

His expression went blank. Stone cold.

"And you know what will happen if you force my hand on this Mags?"

Oh, she knew. "Like you said, I'm willing to do anything for those kids."

Rushing forward, he grabbed her by the neck and shoved her up against the wall. "Back off, Maggie. That's not happening."

His grip was tight, constricting her airway. She felt lightheaded, suddenly.

"Okay. Fine." She choked out.

He squeezed her neck tighter, then released her, knocking her head against the wall. "You may have just saved your life."

"So don't tell the kids, Max." She rested a hand on her throat, still leaning against the wall. "That's fine. But you can't kill me. You know that. The kids are in the next room. And what would they think of you then?"

Max shook his head and walked off. "There is an easy way, Maggie. The one I proposed. Quit making this difficult."

"Tell Lily about us."

He whirled back. "What?"

"Tell Lily about us. Your family in the states. Then I'll back off."

"She already knows."

"Really? Does she know everything, Max?"

He glared into her eyes. Maggie held steadfast. She refused to move even a fraction of an inch.

"I'll tell her, Max, if you don't."

Slowly, his face broke into a wide grin. "Right. Like you could find her."

Maggie waited a few seconds, letting them trip by like silent heartbeats. "Her name is Lilly Colling. She lives on Macleay Island, on Coorong Street... Brisbane, Australia."

Look for *The Me I Left Behind: Maggie's Story*
Coming in 2025

About the Author

Madeleine Jaimes is the women's fiction pen name for bestselling romance author Maddie James.

While Maddie dabbles with cowboys and small town happily-ever-afters, Madeleine explores the real-life, complicated relationships of women, men, and families, and tackles those problems through story. She figures she's lived long enough to bring some of her own life experiences into the mix.

Maddie also writes mainstream romantic suspense as M.L. Jameson.

Maddie James and pen names have published over 70 romance titles worldwide, and in a variety of formats (ebook, print, audiobook, and more). Affaire de Coeur says, "James shows a special talent for traditional romance," and RT Book Reviews claims, "James deftly combines romance and suspense, so hop on for an exhilarating ride."

Learn more at www.maddiejamesbooks.com